String Horses

Ursula Holden

London Magazine Editions
1976

Also by Ursula Holden

Endless Race

SBN 904388 11 5

Printed in Great Britain by
Unwin Brothers Limited
The Gresham Press, Old Woking, Surrey, England
A member of the Staples Printing Group

Cast a cold eye
On life, on death.
Horseman, pass by

W.B. YEATS

1

'Joanna, please. Start it once again. You dream. A harmonic scale does not descend in the minor key.'

'I keep forgetting.' Joanna shook the spit from her recorder. She tried to put feeling into her blowing. The more she felt, the wetter, flatter were the notes. Her elbows drooped, her sweaty fingers slipped over the holes. Her lips ached. The lesson always started by her thinking she was a girl wonder, would astonish the world. After half an hour of play it seemed less likely. Miss Delicate said that she didn't practise enough. A slack attitude to practice meant a slack performance.

'I do practise quite a lot. At home.'

'It is a question of approach. The recorder is demanding. You must give it all. A scale must receive the care of a cadenza. Now, Joanna, keep those elbows up.'

The music on the stand was open at a sonata for piano, woodwind and strings. Miss Delicate raised her fiddle with a shower of resin, her bow and finger-board were white with it. She persuaded herself that her words were true, that Joanna needed special lessons on an instrument that some called lowly; a whistle only fit for children's lips. She tackled the passage like a workman, ending with a flourish. Fresh resin fell. Sound bounced from the walls of the little room. Miss Delicate was well built. She played with feet apart. She believed in posture.

'It's so hot.' Joanna didn't like to say that Miss Delicate's playing was out of tune. The room, the heat, the distracting sunshaft full of motes added to the distortion. There was barely room for two, one fiddling, one blowing, beside the piano. She loved Miss Delicate; her thoughts rarely strayed from her; but it was a secret love, because the other girls would laugh. Miss Delicate was old, beloved by Joanna for want of anyone else. She dreamed of rescuing her from leprosy or flu, memorised her remarks and tried to please her by playing brilliantly.

Miss Delicate had never been a beauty. She waved her large hands at Assembly and spoke about the world of art, integrity and weathering storms. It was rare to hear a sound that wasn't ugly coming from the practice room with slime-green walls. Miss Delicate taught music throughout the school, individually and in groups, as well as other subjects. She was mocked.

'Your sister Hope is coming for her singing next, is she not?'

Hope was the beauty of the school, the elder confident sister, who rattled the keys of the piano inaccurately and was having voice-training. Her rendering of 'Hark! Hark! the Lark' was memorable. She was fond of pop songs too. Lucky Hope, skinny, elegant, who had never been known to put herself out for a living soul. Hope was almost seventeen. Separated by eleven months, they were nearly twins. People thought that queer – almost twins – and speculated about their parentage, whether one sister had been adopted, or if the father had been randy. They looked alike, except that Joanna was awkward, less confident than Hope.

'Come, let us round off the lesson with the presto. To the pianoforte.' A good child, a worthy child, but Joanna would remain pedestrian, would never fly like sister Hope. Hope was a girl apart. Might she perhaps harbour a drop of royal blood? Hope might make a mark in the world of art: the responsibility was almost too thrilling to contemplate. Miss Delicate bent over the keys, hammering through the presto. She liked to lift her hands as high and often as possible, sometimes missing sections out. She sat against the treble register, when necessary leaning in a curve towards the base, with rather a swooning face. A younger girl, Euphemia Draye, had once cried out in Assembly that Miss Delicate had fainted, but it was only a long phrasing in the base.

Joanna blew as best she could through her spitty pipe, before wrapping it away in a scarf and laying it in a case. She wouldn't talk alone with Miss Delicate for a week.

Hope came in, but gave no sign of seeing her, leaning against the wall with lids lowered, making sure that Joanna's recorder case didn't brush her. Her lashes were dark, a contrast to her hair, which in sunlight was the colour of hot custard. Today she had arranged it to lie in a tail between shoulder blades, to keep her long neck cool. Hope hated the practice room, a dirty box-like place. Hope liked space. As

8

Joanna left she pushed the sonata to the floor repudiatingly, putting her Lark song in its place. She wished good afternoon to Miss Delicate, her pink lips moving prettily over her large even teeth. Her jaw was well defined. She was ready to render sweet and rounded notes at the striking of Miss Delicate's chord. She was a thoroughbred.

'Now Hope, The Lark. And remember Joanna, practise your scales. Work, work, and anything can happen. Genius is only one percent inspiration.' Genius ah genius. She'd been blowing on sparks, looking for flames of genius for nearly fifty years. She would not weaken.

Joanna wiped her hand on her skirt. She wasn't sure if 'anything' meant entering for public examinations, or the platform of the Albert Hall. Her hands left marks on her dress. Even in cold weather they sometimes steamed. Hope never sweated and condemned the use of deodorants. Hope did nothing to excess, had nothing in defect, though her confidence was immoderate. Her periods gave little trouble. Her proportions were grecian, her underarms downy-soft. A simple action appeared magnetic when performed by Hope. She painted her nails a filmy green, rubbed lemon lotion into her calves. She was vain of her long thighs and small breasts. Annoyances like spots, sweat, grease round chin and nostrils, clumsy feet and elbows were unknown to her. Hope was not burdened with love for anyone but herself. But she needed Joanna's love as she needed food, it was a dependence, though she never acknowledged her during school. She skimmed through her days on a breeze, singing wide-mouthed, letting forth her rather breathy soprano.

'Before you leave Joanna, open the window', Miss Delicate called forgetting that the sashcord was broken. She owned the school; penny-pinching had become a way of life. She was never free from worry. Her nights were sleepless from the worry of how to make ends meet. Parents of the kind of girl she wished to illumine expected qualified staff; staff of this calibre demanded salaries to match. So Miss Delicate was forced to take on more and more herself, to force fragments of fact from a memory becoming increasingly dim. Dancing, music, poetry were her subjects; tools with which to guide a chosen few into the world of art. Such things as account books, gym shoes, coke for the boiler, essays about trade winds were sordid. She was happy teaching music to one or two, to Hope or Lavender

Charger. Dear Joanna, a girl at her most glandular age, was a useful pupil because she took a lot of extras. Recorder lessons, watered orange juice at break, French coaching with Madame were items outside the school curriculum.

She settled over the keys, her fiddle put aside, her linen dress billowing over the stool. She wore hand-woven frocks in colours washed to insignificance. Her clothes were shapeless, fitting her heavy limbs loosely.

Noises of tennis-playing came through the shut window, mingling with the music. Shouts of 'fifteen love', 'Gosh, well played Lavvie', 'Deuce', made a backing to Hope's huge breaths. 'Hark! Hark! the lark at heaven's gate sings, And Phoebus 'gins arise, His steeds to water at those springs On chalic'd flowers that lies.'

Hope and Lavender Charger were rivals, heading different factions. Hope wished that Joanna was a sister to be proud of. Because of Joanna Lavender pitied her. Joanna was worse than a freak, tagging in the shadows with her mouth drooping. She ignored the heat in the practice room as she sang, rocking on her heels as a prima-donna might. She was fond of her voice. Miss Delicate, hurling her large body up and down the keys in pursuit of her hands, was equally happy.

Outside the slime-green door Joanna hesitated. She was a natural eaves-dropper. Listening to people saved you from being involved with them. She had heard Hope and Lavender laughing about her bust in the Cloaks.

In the adjoining room, little larger than a cupboard sat Madame correcting French. Musical instruments lacking vital parts and stationery were also kept there. Madame was given to whispering. Used to being put upon, she didn't complain of her quarters, she was glad of the post. She had to work from the light of a thirty watt bulb in the corridor.

'Child, child, don't ever fly', she whispered. This caution came often to her lips: some said she'd lost a loved one in the skies during World War One. She had the face of a mouse, her wrinkles scrubbed to an ivory shine. Advising people not to fly made her less agitated. She layered herself in shawls and nibbled cracker biscuits from a cigar box.

The practice rooms were good for secret meetings. Girls crouched there during break and smelled the resin, dust, apple cores and Madame's crackers. Prospective parents were told about the Music Annexe, but not shown there. Miss Delicate stressed her aim to encourage the Arts – Music and the Dance in particular. The number of her pupils remained small. It was her dream to form a choir fit to enter Festivals. She resented her time being spent in teaching Geography and Science to save staff fees. She lived in dread of visits from the Educational Inspector, who might report her for false representation. Entries for public examinations were nil, in spite of claims on her prospectus. So Miss Delicate worried nightly about cheese-paring and Inspectors, as well as dreaming of orchestras, free expression and the emergence of prodigies. The going was hard.

Madame gave a sneeze. She held her page to the light. She blinked as she heard Miss Delicate sing with Hope, hitting a note at a crescendo, their combined sounds not attractively matched.

'What are you waiting for Joanna?'

'Nothing. Nothing, really. I'm waiting for my sister Hope.'

'But she has only just gone in. Go now, to what you should be studying. Don't fly.'

'It's a free period. There's nothing more till four o'clock.'

Miss Delicate disliked idleness. She liked her girls to keep on the move, the older ones to supervise the young, to tidy kitchen premises, help the Major with extra Maths, assist one another to limber up in the Remedial room, or outside on the court. Grace would not be acquired without limbering. One of Miss Delicate's idols was Isadora Duncan. She wanted her girls to form a dancing band. Every morning she put them to heaving and hoisting their limbs to the count of four, freely expressing themselves. In all weathers they bent and postured, following Miss Delicate's method. She believed that the body could be contorted to shape each letter of the alphabet. Some, like the letter O were hazardous. Fat limbs wove, thin limbs strove to reach a letter, spell a simple word, to shape out some meaning. Joanna felt unhappy about this practice; Miss Delicate was making a mistake. The rest considered it a lark, and that no time spent in school was to be taken seriously. It was a happy place, with homework kept to a minimum. Homework meant marking, there were few qualified to do this. So girls left Hoaley Academy much the same as they had entered it, speaking nicely, having learned a few poems, sums and French songs.

They left to wait at home for men to come along and give them similar homes, with a garage, dish-washer and creeper round the porch. They were not ambitious. School dinners were frightful.

Twice a week a retired Major came to teach Maths. Miss Delicate enjoyed her own subjects, it was the subjects that she neither knew nor understood that were so tiresome. At night she worked on her manuscript. 'Gertrude V. Delicate's Alphabetical Posturing.' She would patent her method.

She provided her pupils with chalk, as paints were costly. Sometimes she made the younger ones scratch on the paths, like prehistoric men using their cave walls. She liked to see them humping on their knees. A cheap way of expression. Everyone jeered at her, except for Joanna who loved her in spite of her age and silliness. Euphemia quite liked her too. Miss Delicate debased herself for her ambitions which was brave. Other girls loved pop stars or had crushes on grammar school boys the other side of Putney Bridge. These passions were discussed in the practice rooms and Cloaks. Those who had no crush admired Lavender or Hope. Lavender was reputed to be wild, would catch a millionaire. Hope Greenham had style and elegance. No one knew of Joanna's affection for the Head. She wrote her poems in the lavatory, flushing them away because they were no good.

At the end of the Annexe was the main corridor leading to the Cloaks. The tennis-players were pushing.

'Tanned skin is commonplace. I don't mean you, naturally, Lavvie darling.'

'Do you mind? This racquet is new. Careful.'

'We should have won. I strained my wrist.'

'The Greenham sisters look alike, I will admit. They're different in behaviour. Oh hullo Joanna. Jo, did you know that Mallory fancies your big sister?'

'What do you mean?'

' "What?" she says. Mallory fancies Hope. I've seen him staring. We've all noticed it. 'Course she is lovely, I will admit.' Lavender could afford to be magnanimous, she had a boy, a friend of her brother, who was soft about her.

'I didn't know.'

'What Joanna didn't know, she didn't want to know.' Lavender

12

thanked the Lord she had no sister like Joanna. The Chargers were a normal family. Her brother was an asset. Her parents stayed together.

Joanna wiped her hot hands on the roller towel. Every day she wished that Hope would walk home with her. It never happened. When lessons were over the girls gathered in the Cloaks to listen to Hope and Lavender outdoing one another.

'Oh Hope, do you know that you have inspired passion in the caretaker's breast?'

Hope smiled. She knew the value of not answering. She went to the basin to pat her long throat with cool water. She had sung well. She looked in the mirror, admiring her thin fingers and white throat. At the base of her fingers the skin grew in a curious web-like way. In certain positions her fingers were like the cartilaginous bones of a fish. Confident of her looks she gave the impression that those who lacked webs were the odd ones. She pulled her mouth into various shapes, this way, that. Her firm jaw belonged to a doer, not a dreamer like Joanna. She flipped her hair free, fanning her neck, then walked over to change into her coloured sandals. Her feet stayed nice in all weathers. Hers were the longest legs in the school.

'Did you hear Hope? The caretaker is after you.' Lavender looked at her own sun-burned face and black curls. She kept her smile. Hope was a bitch. Hope was in love with her own white-skinned fish-handed image.

'Oh that. Attractive isn't he? A dish, really.'

' "Dish" she says. A dish rather past his prime. Fine, if you like your meat well-hung.'

'Didn't you know that I drive men wild Lav?' Hope looked at Lavender's tan and pitied her. She pitied the schoolboys that tagged after her. Lavender was immature.

'Hope, I say, shall we walk home? When you're ready, I mean.'

Worse than refusal was not being acknowledged, as if she didn't exist. Worst of all was the giggling of Euphemia Draye, watching Joanna push her recorder case into her satchel. Recorder-playing was jeered. She was the only one who knew the truth, that Hope had no boy wild about her, not even a boy to pay her bus fare home, and that she worried about it quite a lot. Hope encouraged the belief that she was a femme fatale. A fifth-former should have someone, if only a

13

cousin, someone to pay for coffees, cinemas, or trips along the river. Once at home she and Hope lead cut-off lives, relying on each other exclusively for company. School and home, though only separated by Putney Bridge and two street-lengths, were worlds apart. Hope blamed Joanna for handicapping her chances with boys.

Joanna envied the younger sisters of elder ones who let them carry satchels, bought them toffee apples, or helped with homework. The Greenhams walked apart, one behind the other, over Putney Bridge. They teased Joanna, called her Hope's little dog. Girls were in awe of Hope. They listened to her and Lavender, made smarmy remarks and tried to copy them.

Joanna left the Cloaks, walked past the tennis court to where Mallory was oiling the gate. It was a shock to learn of his interest in Hope. Her heart felt too big, a swollen feeling. School was bad enough, she only managed to bear it by loving Miss Delicate through the day. Now, her home security with Hope was threatened by the figure in the overall.

He swung the hinges back and forth, the oil-can on the ground between his shoes. He hadn't worked at Hoaley Academy for long, was still an object of speculation by the girls, the only male who came there every day. The Major taught Maths twice a week. There was poor Geld, a pensioner who helped in the kitchen. The day-to-day running of the school depended on Mallory, who, posted by the gate, was waiting for another glimpse of Hope. Joanna watched him. She wondered if he had noticed her bust. He had an experienced face, lumpy-lipped, and a nose that slanted slightly to the left. His eyes were hazel shading into green, they noticed every girl as she walked through his gate. His scalp showed through in places, though he brushed his hair over to touch his overall, white now, for summer. The open air had tanned his neck and hands. His eyes were his best feature, looking with a serious brown-green glance as though used to distant spaces. Euphemia Draye came by, a loner like Joanna. She, too, lived on the other side of the Bridge. She was backward, and had attacks of hayfever. The sight of Mallory made her fiddle for her nasal spray. He was strong, an outdoor person, he had an effect on all. Hayfever, giggling, pushing with uncontrolled cries occurred when Mallory was near. The gate hinge squeaked as Hope and Lavender came through the door. Hope had pinioned her hair by a

14

rubber band to lie in a swatch in front of one shoulder. She knew that next day others would imitate this unusual style. She kept her face turned towards Lavender, knowing that Mallory and Joanna were watching.

'Joanna can't hold a racquet, much less hit the ball', she said. It was a lie. At home they knocked balls against the garden wall, enjoying it in friendliness. At school Joanna wouldn't play because the girls were cruel. They liked you to muff a shot.

'She is a problem alright. Poor fish', Lavender said, noticing Joanna near the gate.

'You see, you're lucky Lav. You don't have to share your things. A younger sister is inhibiting. She sleep-walks too.'

Lavender smiled. Her lips were usually wet from gossiping and smiling unkindly. During holidays she went on cruises or skiing trips. She kept snapshots in her pencil box of skiing instructors, or Swedes with towels, lying on their stomachs. Lavender relied on her reputation for fastness, she knew about drugs and orgies. It annoyed her that Mallory hadn't singled her out, preferring her enemy. He was an enigma. Girls said he'd been an officer and been seconded. Had been titled, lost his all at cards. A priest, a spy, a policeman who took bribes. His hands were deft as they oiled the hinges. In the sun his thick brows looked an almost foxy red. As each girl went by him he said 'Off home now?' or 'Be good sweet maid' in a roguish voice, as though for a price he'd like to hang them with diamonds. Each time he flattened his cheeks into a smile a girl was made to giggle and wriggle. The young ones lost control, pushed each other with baskets of books and blushed. Pink-cheeked or pale, greasy-haired or dandruffy, long-nailed or bitten, all wanted his attention. Some dropped balls near his feet.

Lavender made a forehand drive at him with her racquet, pushing her lips forward in a kissy way. Hope looked down. Her long eyes were her best point, with bluish whites, as though each iris had run. They were wideset, with drooping outer corners, giving a look of vulnerability. She experimented with colouring and various brushes. Sometimes her eyes were works of art. It was exciting to feel Mallory's hand brush hers, exciting that he fancied her. The experience was new and frightening. He mended things, oiled locks, banged nails into heavy pieces of furniture, yet his fingers had felt smooth. He

15

helped Miss Delicate wherever he was needed: he was well-suited to the name of handy man. He was easy-going, would call the register, supervise revision, had taken first form Maths when Major was away. It was certainly boosting to her ego to be singled out.

'The poor fish hankers after Miss Delicate. It must be shaming for you Hope.'

'She what? Miss Delicate?'

'She wrote "I love Miss Delicate" on her rubber. I saw. Is she changing her sex, or what?'

Lavender didn't wait after this salvo. She went through the gate in the direction of the local Wimpy Bar, to be admired by boys for her sexiness and indulge her love of buns stuffed with raw mince.

The pupils of Hoaley Academy were insulted by the local children. They gathered at bus stops in clumps, to shout 'Diddums, where's your chuvver?' and 'Ponce.' Girls came to Miss Delicate from various localities, drawn by the status of a private school. Few had aspirations to the world of Art. The place could look pretty in summer, with wistaria, laburnum trees and wall flowers round the tennis court. Flowers drew the eye from broken stucco and damp patches. When creepers crawled over paint and warped window-frames, it was time to show a parent round. Miss Delicate could then extol the beauty of a garden, keeping away from the dangerous subject of exams. They watched the girls banging tennis balls over the net, admired the blossom, listened to a note or two coming from the Annexe. In school the girls were carefree. They scattered once out of school.

Joanna watched Hope get on the bus. She got on one behind her, her spirits low because of Lavender and the rubber. Joanna scribbled on anything, on hankies, table-tops and on her forearm whenever she imagined involvements in which Miss Delicate relied on her. The charm of loving the Head was knowing that your dreams would never happen. You could indulge freely. She saw Hope's hair ahead, a beacon. The buses moved jerkily over the bridge.

Inside their square red brick house they could resume their home relationship, become sisters again. It took a minute to adjust.

'What is this rubbish then? What have you been writing? Not content with hanging round open-mouthed you have to be a sexual freak.'

'It was a joke Hope.'

'Joke my bum. Lavender didn't think so. She pities me. Your behaviour doesn't do me any good.'

'But you don't like Lavender. Why should you care what she says?'

'It the best policy to be friendly. I placate the enemy. Stuck-up sow.' To think of Lavender made Hope sick. Her cruises, joss sticks, ski-suits and accounts of conquests. Boys went for her.

'And what is this about Mallory?'

'He's twice as good as Lavender's schoolboys. The whole school drools over him.' Mallory would never paw her skirts under Wimpy Bar tables, or whistle at her from corners.

'But he's the Caretaker.'

'So? I like the look of him.' She liked his hands; they were so capable. She could see him as a surgeon, stitching bodies after accidents. He was like the gamekeeper in *Lady Chatterley's Lover* – a favourite character. Better to love a Caretaker than scribble notes of love to the Head. There was nothing wrong with Mallory.

'I'd hate to think what *she* would say.'

'She wouldn't care. When is she coming in?' Hope asked.

They referred to their mother as 'she', united by their shared dislike. A mother who put work before her children was unworthy of the name.

'It's a lecture night.'

'She wouldn't care if she came home and found us dead. She'd love it. She'd be free.'

'I shouldn't think she'd mind much.'

Having a Family Planning consultant for a mother was worse than having none. Uniting against her cemented their loving friendship while indoors. They gave her no quarter. Her work of preventing life kept her for long hours in clinics and lecture halls. While advising her sex in methods of child prevention, she neglected her own. School differences were forgotten in their common hatred of her. Her absence made them dependent and fond. They didn't know the neighbours, they turned to one another, true sisters once inside their door. They liked to kiss each other lightly, to fondle, push each other with taunts. 'You prat-faced les. Get off.' Each afternoon they removed their frocks in the hall, the evidence of school, ripping at buttons and sandal buckles, chucking things over the floor. Then they were free. When frocks came off school melted from the mind. Their

17

striped dresses, turquoise, lime or mulberry were kicked under the oak chest. Shoes followed. Because of her indifference they did just what they liked.

Their mother had agreed to let them go to Hoaley without seeing it. They'd noticed the wistaria and laburnum dropping blossom over the school wall, had peered through the barred gate and liked the look of it. A secret-looking decayed sort of place, not large. 'Miss Delicate?' their mother had questioned. 'You want to study there? Hoaley Academy? Alright. Does she teach tatting? Water colours? Very well. Let it be so.' She'd written out cheques ever since. She never read reports or knew when term began. She was indifferent, unaware if her girls were quick or dull; she thankfully gave Miss Delicate the responsibility and left them alone. She paid the increasingly large bills for extra singing, recorder lessons, fruit, anything Miss Delicate suggested, the money bought her freedom of conscience. The girls decided their own lives, she paid the piper. When home she cleaned the house and tidied, apart from the girls' bedrooms which they locked. She saw the fridge was stocked. Her duty was done. Her girls were looked after, leaving her free for her work. She wasn't told when Hope bought a Belgium hare. She was allergic to animal fur and suffered asthma attacks. The girls hid the rabbit; a secret weapon, ready to be loosed. It hopped out now, nibbling at shoe straps. They agreed that their mother would be unconcerned whether Hope loved Mallory, nor would she notice messages on rubbers.

'She has no interest in men. It's years since Daddy left. I can't remember.'

'Nor can I.'

'Perhaps she gets a kick from examining patients. Talking about it.'

'How awful. I heard her having asthma again last night. The rabbit keeps scratching his ears. It's canker.'

'Have you got the powder?'

'Why should I do it? He belongs to you. Hope, what's that letter?' On the floor by Hope's dress was an envelope.

'I suppose it's another bill. Miss Delicate saving a stamp again. A bill for *her.*'

They were fond of reading other's letters, a bill was better than nothing. A letter, circular or note were evidence of care, attention wanted or received, notes meant that you mattered. Coupons for

18

coffee, notices of carpet sales, tracts from Jehovah's Witness were read with attention. They went through waste baskets, handbags, drawers for scraps concerning their mother and her life. Euphemia poked notes smelling of nasal spray through their front door. She wrote doggerel, and wanted them to praise her efforts. Hope kept a letter from a boy in Cornwall, met once on St. Ives beach. It said he would remember her with loving thoughts. They were two ships passing at night. This note stayed in her knicker drawer to be read and re-read. Hope was the most inquisitive in regard to their mother's desk. While Joanna copied poems she went scrupulously through the desk. These pastimes were hobbies. Quiet safe evening followed quiet safe evening. Sometimes they spent the night on the sofa, after the late night movie had finished. Their mother slept in hotels when lecturing far away.

'Such ornate script', Hope said. ' "Signed from yours E.M." Who on earth is that?'

'It must be for you. It's from that beastly Mallory.'

'I thought his christian name was Mallory. What a snob Miss Delicate must be to use his surname without Mister.'

'Miss Delicate is not a snob. She is most liberal.' Joanna thought of Miss Delicate at Assembly, praying her broadminded prayers, to please all pupils. Though Humanist, she had an interest in Islam, moon research and Orphism. Miss Delicate seeking for luminaries to further the world of Art would never belittle an employee. 'Read it Hope.'

' "Dear Hope. I have something you might like. Come and see me during break. You know where I will be. Signed from yours E.M." Good god, what cheek.'

'Will you go?'

'I shouldn't think so.' But this was from an adult. No snooty love-note from a boy on a Cornish beach, but the genuine thing. Lavender had nothing to equal it.

Joanna moved away. The tiles of the hall felt cold to her soles. The hall was cold. 'Signed from yours E.M.' The rabbit in the kitchen scratched. White fur flew from it's infected ears to settle glintingly on the floor. His back leg worked like a piston. His ears were Hope's responsibility. On the table was a pie, ready for heating. Hope was sought after. 'Signed from yours E.M.' A man had written Hope a note. The caretaker wanted to strike up with her, to have an assignation. In the pan on the stove were sprouts, their stalks notched with criss-cross knife-marks. Flies buzzed under the light. Over the sink she could see a dog through the window, rolling by the letterbox. The tap dripped. An adult person looked at Hope with serious intent. 'Signed from yours E.M.' The Guardian was folded by the pie. The girls disliked reading newspapers, except for television programmes. They never read of wars or violence, were unsure where Vietnam was or what was happening in Ireland. They hated dogs, it pleased them to think of dogs in moon orbit. Joanna collected pictures of Pope John and mourned him when he died. They wished Marilyn Monroe was alive. Pope John was a trustworthy man. Their home closeness was menaced by that note. She threw the pie, sprouts and newspaper into the bucket, got butter from the fridge, cutting a bar of it in two.

'What are you doing? Fudge? I wonder what the "E" is for. His writing is like monks' writing. Let's make it chocolatey, with walnuts.' The sprouts were walnut-shaped, tight and perfect as her own breasts which Mallory had eyed. He dotted his 'i's' with circles. You could imagine insects, animals, hiding in his capitals. He wrote on awful paper. The letter was a talisman. The melting butter smell of fudge was lovely. The Guardian held the pie together in the bucket like a printed plate. Journalists loved disaster. Strikes, murder, Irish bombings, Vietnam and unsuccessful trips to the moon were their delight. 'Joanna why are you so gloomy?'

'I'm not gloomy. You might help me. I do the cooking, I see to your blasted rabbit. Anyhow what does Mallory think he'll give you?'

Hope smiled. She wetted a finger, dipping it in sugar. It maddened Joanna to see her eyelids droop again to read the presumptious scrawl. She felt the rabbit by her ankle. But for her it's ears would be worse.

'How should I know what he has?'

'If you go and talk to him, he'll expect something back.'

'Not jealous by any chance? I may not go. I give nothing that I cannot spare.'

'As I should know. What about last Christmas?' Joanna had given Hope a set of books by D.H. Lawrence. Hope, on Christmas morning, had produced some hankies that she had from Euphemia Draye. Straight from the sneezing hands of Euphemia she'd only altered the label, had laughed at Joanna's disappointment, and finished Lady Chatterley in a day.

'Is it time for testing yet? Don't stir so hard. That splash burned me.'

Routine established itself. They bickered over the fudge, breathing its smell, eating it hot, dumping the pan into the sink, measuring fresh ingredients. The letter became chocolate-speckled. They sipped cups of water to stop from getting sick.

'Do you think he is sincere, Hope? Is Mallory honourable?'

'What does that matter? What does honour have to do with it? It's romance.'

'Will you tell Lavender?'

'Not yet. Lavender can shit herself.' Rude words popped out when she thought of Lavender in her home. The Chargers would be sitting at their meal. Checked table cloth, napkins, croissants in a basket, Daddy there, Lavender's Mama producing something savoury from the stove. Her brother would tease, ask Lavender if she wanted to go out. Enquiries would be made about her school day. Hope looked at the curly fudge-spattered writing again. The dog outside had gone. Soon the daisies on the lawn would shut and they would stop making batches of fudge. The flies had gone. They felt a little sick, in spite of the water. It was cooler. Obviously Mallory had never been an officer. She took a towel to drape round her shoulders, gave Joanna another. They rinsed their hands from the same jet of cold water, long fingers interweaving. Joanna felt Hope's webbed parts. They grinned at each other through fudgy teeth. The charm of sweet-making was its randomness. They never measured, never washed out pans. They hid them underneath the sink, leaving crockery for their mother. It was her job to run the house. The rabbit hopped behind them as they went up to their rooms. Their books would be unpacked, to be replaced untouched next day. It was their routine. The draining board was covered with cups containing samples, toffee trails, rock-hard chunks, greenish sludge floating in water, all part of their fudge routine.

Hope had her piano in her room. At home she played songs that she liked better than those of Miss Delicate's choice. 'Everyone's Gone to the Moon' had a tricky accompaniment. She rippled her fingers, not touching the keys at the worst parts.

21

Joanna sat on her bed. She looked out at the plane tree under which the pillar box stood. It was a pity that her poems came out disappointingly. She'd like to write one about birds, a rare species, a black-throated warbler alighting. She blew a note on her recorder. The rabbit jumped up on her eiderdown. Blood lined the folds of it's ears into which they poked a nozzle of powder from a puffer pack. Later they would watch the movie. Late movies were their strongest bond. They cast a spell on the sisters, leaving them relaxed, nostalgic for the lives they'd shared, reluctant to resume their normal lives. Life in a movie was preferable to real life, especially an old movie, when a happy ending was a certainty.

When Hope had finished her song she went quietly to her mother's room. Joanna didn't feel the same need to know what went on in the planned families, the urge to know which patient had conceived in error, who had switched from pill to coil and who complained of nausea or side effects. She liked to know whose husband was cold and who had hysterectomies. As well as these things there were statements from the bank, or news about their father, resident now in Florida and married to another. Perhaps he'd get more children. A titbit such as that was quarry. Alone, she carried out these checks, leaving no scrap unread. Joanna didn't like the desk. She didn't like the sample pessaries and condoms, the impedimenta of their mother's trade. Hope took them happily from their wrappings. That night she found a tin, the label torn off in the corner. Their mother had written 'Self' in print and inside was a diaphragm. She took it out, held it to the light, bent it back and forth. She heard Joanna piping on her whistle. She dug her nail into the rubber, before putting it in the tin. She said nothing of this discovery.

'We'll use *her* bathsalts', she said, turning on the taps.

Getting into shared baths was another evening ritual. Washed bodies and daily clean clothes were vital, though they were indifferent to a dirty bath or saucepans, nor did they dream of hand-washing after visits to the lavatory. Insults flew when in the bath. It was their closest time of day. Soap shot from hand to hand, mouths twisted in invective. When lathering was finished they settled down. They wedged their toes into each other's armpits and got out their important work. Equipment was kept under the bath, pencils, paper and peppermints. They worked on drawings and poems, breathing hard, crunching sweets, their work lying on folded towels along the bath's edge. The steam and minty taste made a background for great works. Sometimes they sang. The rabbit waited in the corner. Soon the floor was littered. They showed no interest in each other's work, once finished the page was screwed up under the bath. The singing was interrupted by the lap of water round their knees, the slop of flannel and soap, the hot tap going on again. Joanna wrote about birds in cages. Hope drew horses. They didn't expect the arrival of their mother.

2

The rabbit jumped as the door below was banged. They heard the cistern being flushed and then the noise of the sink being filled. The crockery that they'd left was angrily rattled. They lay in the water looking amazed; their mother was supposed to be staying the night in Virginia Water after her lecture there.

'Girls, girls, please hurry out of there. I'm quite worn out. I want a bath and food.'

The sound of her voice quite numbed them, as though they had been doped. They threw the rest of the paper and their pencils out of sight. Steam and the pleasures of the bath had dulled their minds. What a nuisance she was, old hornrimmed woman, disturbing them, breaking into their private world, invading their sisterhood. The rabbit scratched again. They got out of the bath.

'Oh come on you two. D'you hear?' She rose at dawn to wash and tidy for them. She ensured that there was adequate nourishment, she paid those bills for the Delicate institute: a blitzed kitchen and a locked bathroom were her reward. She was a slave to two sluts.

They didn't speak as they moved down the passage, draped now in soaking towels. The doctor would have liked to chat, after she'd rested and had hot tea. A chat, and news exchanged. She didn't know their likes and dislikes, she never received their confidence. She'd like a girly talk. But the two girls moved away like drugged druids, leaving behind five towels on the floor and steam fog-thick. The mirror was spattered with toothpaste, sweet papers plugged up the drain. She'd given birth to sluts. If she hadn't been conscious at the birth she'd say they belonged to someone else. They didn't resemble her ex-husband. How could blood of hers be so rude? Where was equality? They bled her white of cash and care, they sapped her energy, giving nothing in return. Couldn't they be loving? Motherhood was a confidence trick. Was it asking too much that they recognise her existence? Other families joked, planned surprises, made each other

24

trays to eat in bed. She had feelings. She'd like occasionally to doodle sketches, hum and bang a bit on Hope's piano. Hobbies and interests should be shared with smiles, respect. Hope kept her door locked. She'd never put a finger on the piano. They hadn't looked at her, their eyes had blanked as they had crept out from the bath, robed in towels. Without her glasses she couldn't swear but she thought she'd seen something resembling a dog or monkey, white with pricked ears following them. A dirty white four-legged beast. Fur gave her asthma, made her breathless. Sluts.

'Shut the door. There'll be no movie now', Joanna said. They'd both been looking forward to watching *Stolen Life.*

'She's cunning. Sneaking in and disturbing us. I hate her. Why did she come back? The evening's ruined.' Hope took Joanna's scissors and cut the india rubber, shredding 'love' and 'Delicate' into scraps, bending the pieces, cutting them again, with furious snips.

'Watch out, Hope. What are you doing with my rubber. Stop it.'

'It's bloody stupid. Why did you write that on your rubber? I hate that woman in the bathroom. Spoiling things.'

'Poor fool, I expect she muddled up her diary.' Joanna felt virtuous in excusing her. Their mother didn't deserve consideration. She never considered them. 'What's wrong with your eye, Hope? It's jumping. It's the nerve, twitching. Put your finger on it.'

Dr. Greenham splashed herself. She tried to whistle to keep up her spirits. Sluicing the body helped restore the humour. Begone white coat and instruments, begone the rubber glove and notes. How nice to put on something floating, to nibble at a dish prepared by one of those girls locked in the bedroom. They whispered, shut away, she couldn't hear what. They preferred the company of their dog or monkey, after all her trouble to get home early. Her eyes were bloodshot from overwork. She'd scarcely a thread of grey, yet she felt aged. The sink had been full as usual, her expensive pie in the bucket. Sluts. How often she had told her patients 'Don't be a martyr. An unselfish mother breeds a selfish child.' Her own truth faced her. She was confronted by two druids and a monkey in her own home that she slaved to keep. 'Make pals with them', she told her ladies, 'Get on their wave-length'. With soup in bowls before the television, everybody cosy in their nightgowns. Experiment with hair perhaps, some sewing and a joke. She'd been received with little love. Sluts.

The girls whispered. Hope admitted that she envied Lavender to the point of murder. Her family were normal. No wonder she was totally assured. Lavender flaunted her toast-coloured tan, threaded her frizzy hair into innumerable plaits, could shout 'Cool it Man' into Miss Delicate's mystified face. Lavender was deliberately cruel, she was rich. She had the confidence that came from a home with two parents who loved her.

'Don't tell about the note. Ignore it. Ignore Lavender. She's shallow and insipid.'

'But we can't live on like this for ever. Night after night with a rotten rabbit. We can't be solitary for ever.'

Hope didn't want to die a virgin. Lavender hinted at a full experience, her face brown and secretive. Mallory's letter made a crack in the dull pattern of their lives. Joanna was a frightened baby, but she felt that life was passing her, that she must grab chances.

'Girls, girls, shall we go down? I'll make some Bovril.'

'Don't answer. She'll go away. She'll go to her desk and work.' She'd touch the tin marked 'Self'. It wasn't only the note that changed things, the tin had shocked her. She would never hunt in their mother's desk again. She had grown older.

'But, Hope, what's wrong with life at home? It's school that I can't stand.' Her crush on Miss Delicate would be publicised, they'd hear about the rubber. Things would get worse. Mallory ought to be reported.

'Girls, have you got some animal in there? Open, please.' Dishes, hostility, monkeys. She had her allergy to think of. She needed rest. She'd worked herself ill while still bearing the scars of a divorce. Nothing went right; the druids ignored her.

'I shall go. I'm curious. Life is in a rut.'

'You'll kiss, you mean? You'll kiss Mallory?' When she imagined Mallory alone with Hope, Joanna felt a taste like dirt. Lavender once brought an Indian book to the Cloaks, a sex book that had caused shrieks. Excited giggling and squeals. The pictures were scarey, weird positions, creatures, birds. The girls had crowded. Euphemia had sneezed herself dizzy. Eyes had watered from the intensity of their laughing. Lavender had smiled her spitty smile and said there was lots more than that. It took experience to know. 'Oh don't go, Hope.'

Hope pushed the rubber shavings with her toes. She remembered

26

the coldness of the tin's edge against her fingers, the way the label corner had peeled. 'Don't look so smashed. I feel like some adventure. I'd like to be an astronaut.' She wanted power. She'd like to deal out pain. She said the rabbit's nails could do with trimming. 'Signed from yours E.M.'

They didn't leave the room again. The rabbit stayed at their feet. They didn't mind sharing. They turned over at the same time, like married people.

Their mother was gone when they got down. Their frocks were ironed, their shoes put out. A note on the table asked them to let her know what food they liked if pies were not acceptable. Thanks to her they'd never see *Stolen Life*.

When first they'd come to London they had longed for a mother to kiss them off to school. They envied girls whose dinner money, hankies, pencil cases had been put into their hands, who would be greeted by the same maternal face after four. Now, they were used to their empty house. 'I dreamed that you were dying', Joanna said.

'Dream what you like as long as you don't go walking in your sleep. It's creepy.' Hope never dreamed.

On school mornings their alienation started over breakfast. Hope, sipping coffee, sprinkling currents over wheatgerm, wouldn't look with sisterliness at Joanna until they were in the hall again after school. Not touching or smiling, they would be strangers, living to the pattern that Hope set. Joanna watched her taking pains, adjusting her starched dress. She'd washed her hair again. Once the front door banged behind Hope their severance was complete. It was usual for her to taunt her about sleep-walking before leaving.

It was hot again. Commuters exchanged greetings concerning weather. 'Scorcher.' 'Alright for millionaires.' 'The roses won't say No.' The buses moved in jerks over the bridge in a nose-to-tail line of grimed red. Passengers dismounted to walk across, jostling impatiently. Gulls and curlews flew low over the water, their cries deadened by the traffic. Men were coatless. Bare thighs were still in fashion.

Miss Delicate talked to the Hoaley girls about fashion. A woman's dress showed an attitude to life, she told them gravely. A skirt length was an indication of modesty, though in fact she secretly envied the girls their freedom. They didn't have to economise, could indulge their fancies, bare their young limbs to nature. Her own clothes hampered her when demonstrating her postures. She'd love to prance naked through primroses, but was too old for this pleasure. The shortness of Lavender's and the Greenham sisters' skirts was something to deplore.

Joanna watched Hope's hair glinting through the windows of the bus in front. She dreaded the day ahead. Wheatgerm had spilled into her books. She hadn't packed her pencil box.

Mallory was an early riser. He weeded round the tennis court. Re-marking it was a favourite chore. Each morning he checked to see if the lines needed touching up. It was his pride to see the girls' balls making a puff of white chalk-dust as they bounced. Flowers grew in a well-tended bed by the gate. The Hoaley girls were not a tidy lot, excepting for Euphemia, but no lolly stick or paper lay for long on Mallory's paths. It irked him that all of Miss Delicate's equipment needed replacing. The only tools that he was proud of were his own, his screwdrivers and ratchet, kept in the pockets of his overall. He knew he'd get the job when he first set eyes on the school and noted its condition. The salary was parsimonious. He didn't mind. He wanted work where girls were. One glance at the patched roofs, the leaking gutters, the crumbling pointing, the tools, the broken desks and sashcords and he knew. Without a doubt the job was his. These conditions were his warranty. He offered an address, but references were not necessary. The dreadful state of the school was better than a testimonial. He'd looked Miss Delicate in the eye, had said 'I am a Baptist and not afraid of work.' Neither were acquainted with the mode of worship. She'd offered him the post. The tennis net in holes, the marker with the wobbling wheel, the coke shovel had done the trick. Not many would put up with them. Here, he was his own master. As long as he kept his gentle hands busy there was opportunity in plenty to watch the girls playing or doing their gymnastics. He'd spotted Lavender straight off, a sexy piece, a know-all. He thought those excercises foolish, the body wasn't meant to twist into letters; an 'O' or 'B' were a strain unless you were an acrobat, especially for anyone as old as Miss Delicate or Madame. On the occasions he'd been asked to take the morning callisthenics he'd instructed them to perform simple jumping. To watch the rows of variformed titties leaping was bliss. His work provided for his hobby of watching girls take exercise, at gym, running or ball games. And when he saw Hope Greenham stretch out her lovely arms in the letter 'T' he knew the meaning of true love. Like a misbeliever converted to the faith after a vision, Mallory was converted to love. He saw Hope. He wanted her.

Lavender wore a peace band round her brow.

'Still got your rubber Jo? Still writing messages?' she asked.

'Now Ladies please,' Miss Delicate stood in the doorway of the Cloaks. Long ago her voice used to ring clear, quell riots to silence. Now they took no notice. Apart from Joanna, and Euphemia who was simple, Miss Delicate didn't exist for the girls in the Cloaks who went on screaming, throwing shoes and cups of water over the coat stands.

'Lavender dear, what is that on your head? Not uniform I fear. Hope, do not poke your chin.'

Hope was by the far mirror, her admirers round her. They watched her staring at her reflection, lifting her cheeks in a smile of experiment, stretching her neck, turning sideways, her elbows smelling lemony. She ignored requests to sit next to them in French, to lend them comb or pen. Her green-striped dress was elegant, her hair just right.

'Have you finished Hope? Ladies please, enlightenment awaits.' Miss Delicate sighed. Though they giggled and ate fruit in lessons, though they disobeyed her, she could and she would show them the way, a glimpse into the world of Art. Only last week Lavender had walked the guttering of the gym, tossing her curls in the spring rain, ignoring her 'Ladies please' until the pipe had broken. Mallory had mended it with special paint and bandages, had made new an old and broken thing. Mallory was their knight in armour. The school was going down and few cared. Madame and Major were true-blues. Mallory was loyal. Madame had turned ill when literature of a disgusting nature was found in Lavender's desk.

Years back, when dinners had been hot and meaty, girls had passed School Certificate after lessons that went with a swing. She'd been able to remember dates of kings, parts of speech and the meaning of ordnance survey maps. And the Hoaley accounts had showed a profit. It had been a joy to watch the girls like Hope who waited like vessels to be filled with fine things from the world of Art. Miss Delicate walked in the steps of the Pre-Raphaelites and had a soft spot for the longer haired ones, clothing them in her mind with robes that rustled

29

to the ground. These bare-footed, lily-clasping favourites included Joanna, Euphemia and other lesser lights because their parents had money and paid the bills for extras without question. She planned an extra nature-spotting class. Miss Delicate's clothes were trimmed with saddle-stitching and her stockings were knitted. Each day she read a line of Christina Rosetti. Her posturing was getting painful because of age. Old joints dried. Her ambition to lead like Isadora had to be curtailed to mere praying motions, rotating her wrists while exhorting her young ladies to write messages with their bodies. Lavender refused to remove that object from her head. It grew late. She called and muttered but they took no notice. Hope was her favourite. Hope was ethereal, bestowed with beauty, might succeed. Private tuition on the recorder had been a stroke of inspiration for Joanna. And fruit. These extra fees meant that visits from auditors were not as dread as those from educational inspectors. The Joannas, the Euphemias, whose shoulders sulked beneath a weight of hair and whose abilities were less than average were vital. They had cash.

'Now, Ladies, please. The spirit plus the letter of the law.' She tucked her hands into her trailing sleeves ready to pray her special prayers before rendering songs on the piano in a triumph of rubato. She provided copies of Rosetti, William Morris, Ruskin, but only her own brindled hairs fell into their pages. Other books, disgusting stuff, lured girls away from what was sterling. She didn't dare accuse Lavender outright.

The girls knocked into her. Old fool and her ideas. Gradually they left the Cloaks, except for Hope hiding at the end.

Mallory checked that no stray balls lay among the flowers. Sogginess didn't improve the spring of old balls. The tulips had a bitter smell, their petals pressed against the wire netting, curling through the gaps. The padlock of the gate onto the court was rotted. The wheel of his barrow was split, so that he had to half carry it forward as he moved. He liked weeding and keeping the beds neat. He kept the grass that edged the paths as neat as sliced cake. A tendril of convolvulus twined in and out of his rake. He whistled through his teeth. Soon it would be time to refuel his boiler and have a smoke. He balanced the rake on the barrow, pulling the door behind him.

While the school sang in praise Hope sneaked out to the boiler room. When she breathed the throat-catching stink of fumes she understood why it was strictly out of bounds. Mallory's hidey-hole was unhygenic, dark and dangerous to health.

He had his back to her, shovelling coke into the boiler that kept them warm in winter, fed the hot taps of the Cloaks. His spade was so broken that it buckled as he scraped. He bent to pick up larger pieces with his hands, his white-clad back moving up and down from the floor to the mouth of the boiler. Yellow smoke puffed out as the coke sifted down. It hung round him like melting ribbons. He didn't hear her come.

'Hullo Mallory', she said. 'Hullo.'

He didn't answer, continuing to stoke. She spoke again. Was he deaf or what? She'd been amenable, had come at his beckoning. She was slumming, the least he could do was notice her.

'Ah. I thought you might be coming. Got my note then?'

'Aren't you surprised to see me?'

'I asked you, didn't I?' He had sharp ears. He'd heard her. He'd learned early to conceal surprise, be watchful, think before he spoke. Keep them guessing, cover pleasure or dismay under an offhand manner. He'd waited for days to plant the note. Patience was a valuable asset. He knew of their girlish speculations, their gossiping around the toilets. He was a source of wonder to the girls, and now his chosen one was standing in his coke, just looking at him. She was his moonbeam girl.

'Welcome to my parlour, Hope.'

'Your parlour, as you call it, is out of bounds.' It was a lair, not a parlour. He was too quick to use her christian name. The way he wiped his mouth on his cuff was graceless, his eyes were insolent, glittering at her through the smoke.

'I know it's out of bounds, Hope. But you came, just the same didn't you?'

'Because you asked me.'

'Yes.'

'You said . . ..you said you . . . had something. What?'

He put his spade against the boiler, to feel in the pocket of his coat behind the door. 'It's something that I made. You'll like it. There.'

'What is it? An animal. A little horse. How did you know that I loved horses?'

'I guessed you would.'

31

'It's made of string. A white string horse. It's lovely Mallory. I love it.'

She examined it in the light from the door. Made of tightly plaited string it was small enough to stand in her palm. Its tail frayed out to bush behind, but the body was varnished hard as wood. Its ears were sharp, its hooves and features modelled delicately.

'Glad that you like it then. 'Course they take time to make. You fray it after plaiting. Then you put on the glue and model it while it's tacky.'

'Where did you learn?'

He picked it from her hand, examining it. He smiled, satisfied, and gave it back into her palm. 'I learned to as a boy. Always handy with my hands. I learned it as a lad.'

'Who taught you?'

'An uncle. We was ... we were travellers. My family were travellers.'

'You mean travelling salesmen?'

'No, not that. We travelled. One of my uncles owned a fair. A family concern.'

'When was that?'

'Years back. I left the fairs for steady work when I got older. That's how I come to be here. So you like the horse?'

'I love it. Thanks.'

'I wanted to please you. Something you would like.'

She felt the hooves cutting between her fingers where he pressed them. He said again that he wanted to please her. She asked him if he worked in the ring. A trapeze perhaps, or tightrope?

'A fair isn't a circus. I worked a fair.' Handy with his hands, he'd landed his moongirl. She had his gift in her hand.

'Sideshows do you mean?'

'That's it, Hope. A fair.'

'Tell me. Talk to me about it.' It was lovely having her hands caressed, as if she'd waited all her life for this. She listened while he spoke about the fair and held and stroked her hands. In winter he said, when times were slack he learned to make things, knick-knacks, household decorations.

'Yes. Go on about it.'

'One of the uncles looked after me. There were side-shows.

32

Animals and that.' He'd worked with every kind of animal. Crocodiles could be snappish if you didn't feed them well. He liked the horses best. He'd worked for years with horses, helped to train them. Breaking horses in was another side-line. He was glad he'd pleased her, glad she seemed interested in his faraway life. He felt between her fingers wonderingly. He'd never felt hands like them.

'The girls say that you can't be trusted.' She was getting used to the feel of him. His eyes above her own were shining with friendliness.

'I can be trusted. Trust me Hope. You've got a lovely skin and a lovely neck. A Venus neckline, did you know that?'

'No?'

'A mark like that means you need love. You need to give it and you need it back.' She must be gentled. Gentling was what he knew about. You had to go slow. Cajolery and kindness, he'd learned the trick of it from handling crocodiles and other frightened beasts. This girl would be no trouble. A bit of luck about her Venus neckline.

His touching made her helpless. She felt lassooed. The boiler gave a sort of moan and settled into redness. The smoke had cleared. He moved his fingers from her elbows back down to her hands, then travelled upwards sensitivily. Her neck was gorgeous. He looked at it quite ravenously.

'I was nearly strangled at birth', she said, and gave a laugh. The chord had become entwined and caused alarm.

He didn't smile, but made a crooning sound, touching her neck. He reached his other hand to bolt the door, keeping a grasp on her. He moved his thumbs, feeling the down growing under her arms. His mooney one, compliant, for whom he'd made the horse, would soon be nuzzling him. He hadn't had a ride in ages.

With the door bolted it was quite dark. Hope smelled the smoke that blended with his fresh sweat. His overall felt crisp. Their shoes crunched in the grit as he half pushed, half lifted her across the coke. Behind the boiler was a kind of nest, some newspaper on boxes, covered by a good thick blanket. It was his hideaway for smoking and a rest, where no one could find him. She felt his slanting nose against her pointed one and soon she felt his tongue. His tongue licked messages on hers, a new exciting writing. His handy hands soon moved to her other hairy places, stroking, sending messages of prickly delight. She felt a giddiness as her breathing lengthened. The

33

boiler sighed. He breathed in pants, long serious puffs into her mouth.

He heard the rattling latch before she did. He never forgot to be wary. A person needed to be watchful, the same as being clean or steady with the hands. He took pride in being clean about his person. Though getting passionate he still kept his ears open. He heard the whispering outside the door.

'Hope, come out. Hope, you must come out.'

He had her green lace panties whipped up in a flash. 'Is that that sister of yours? Is she hanging about out there?'

'Joanna? It couldn't be. I never heard her.' She'd got the hang of writing with her tongue, the smokey place was heavenly. She pushed her stomach into him, wanting a bit more.

'Hope, Hope come out.'

'She's not your shadow is she? What's got into her?'

'She worries about me. She can't help it. I shall have to go.'

'Oh no you don't. Come here.'

'I must. She's younger than me. Thank you for the horse.'

'But you'll come back. You'll come again, Hope?'

'Hope, Hope come quickly. The Major is angry.' Joanna's face outside the door was pale.

'The Major? What the bloody hell are you doing here? Spying as per usual? You ruin everything. Complaining about Major when I'm busy.'

'I had to. The Major is in a towering mood.'

'The Major and his moods are unimportant. What ever is that on your leg?'

'He sent me. He called the register and you weren't there. He roared.'

The Major was a man of moods. The girls enjoyed it when he had fits of remembering his byegone days, the days of barracks square and squad drill, when he would look at the rows of feminine faces with disbelief and loathing. Simultaneous equations were no substitute for marching soldiers in the Punjab. These wenches didn't know their tables, let alone how to form fours. Absence, or a loosened puttee were not to be tolerated. Joanna quailed when he shouted. Where was Hope Greenham? Fetch her. Fetch. Rout her out, report to him with pencil at the double. Hurry.

34

'I might have known he would tell *you* to find me. What is that on your leg?'

'I suppose it's pollen. What were you doing, Hope?' She hadn't wanted to go, had not liked following, she was afraid. Listening and prying were engrained in her. She'd leaned against the door, had strained to hear, had waited for sounds. Pollen from the yellow-petalled tulips clung to her legs. She'd heard no 'I love you', no kissing sounds but silence. Beneath the fear and curiosity, beneath her loneliness was the knowledge that Hope wanted her, had hoped that she would follow. She put her ear to the door, waiting for something, a noise, a sign that would include her. Her life was spent in following. The silence in the boiler-room was frightening.

'Mind your own business and get out of my way. Eavesdropper.'

Hope ran past the tennis court, her hand clenched in her pocket.

At four she wasn't in the Cloaks. Lavender asked for her. Without Hope in the Cloaks to compete with, the home-going lacked sparkle. The Putney hall was empty when Joanna got there. Upstairs came Hope's voice from behind her bedroom door. 'Streets full of people, all alone. Roads full of houses, never home. Church full of singing, out of tune: Everyone's gone to the moon.'

There was no shared bath that night. Hope had left a rim of black round the edge. Her green pants, screwed into the bottom of the laundry basket, were blackened with coke dust.

Her string horse was on the piano in her bedroom. Joanna looked at it enviously, observing the hooves lifted in a canter, its teeth barred ready to bite her.

3

The horse marked the time. There was before and after the visit to the boiler room. The horse stood on Hope's piano mockingly, as if it said 'I belong to Hope. I stand for secrets.' Joanna rehearsed speeches, whispering to the taps while in the bath. 'You needn't think I care. You're lowering yourself.' 'That horse is voodoo, you're a stranger.' 'Mallory has made a fool of you. I'll tell Lavender.' Days went by without them speaking. The drawing books and peppermints stayed unused in the bathroom. The bottoms of the fudge pans settled into sludge. She tried to make a horse of her own, but the string broke, she spilled the glue. She asked Hope if she could look at hers, examine it. Hope said that Joanna could bash her brains out for all she cared, but on no account was she to enter her room or touch anything of hers. They didn't watch the television any more.

Hope stayed in her room, re-reading Lawrence and writing notes. She imagined her life with Mallory. She saw herself in a cottage, cooking dinners. Outside he and his horse ploughed the field. After seeing to the beast he'd see to her. Laughter in the firelight. He would make things with his clever hands and play with her. She didn't want to grow apart from Joanna; because of Mallory it had happened. After a specially abandoned fantasy the sight of him was sometimes disillusioning. Dreams blurred the lines of reality. Chagrin made her take it out on Joanna. She hated her, she'd like to kick her teeth in, she hated her for spying, hated her for looking woebegone. She'd kick her teeth in for making her feel guilty. She heard her crying in her sleep. That was the last straw. Joanna was a creep. She wished that Mallory didn't have a country accent.

'Hope must have got the bug. Has she got a bloke on the quiet?' Lavender asked Joanna.

Joanna turned her face away. She remembered the times before they ever came to London, the country days. Until the boiler man and

36

his string horse had come into their lives they had done everything together, it had been so on the farm.

Their mother had said the Village school would do until things were sorted out. She meant until she had adjusted to her state of separation. Their father had been gone for ages. Divorce was pending. The girls and their mother went to the farm to recover from the pain of shattered relationship. She said the Village kids would soon accept them, they'd make friends. It didn't happen. Their clothes, their accents, their lack of any Dad, their Doctor Mum had made them suspect. The little girls were frightened of cattle, wouldn't join in jumping games at school. They didn't understand the playground lore, or what to do in church on Sunday. Names of local eccentrics, the rituals of Christmas, with old men who rang handbells and the Vicar's sing-song were unaccountable. The Village children herded together, threw stones at them. Dislike was mutual. Their mother said 'You're lucky, you have each other, take no notice. Play alone.' Their rooms had been rented from a farmer, whose wife had been kind. She'd let the children watch her bake, but not to touch; flour on those pretty clothes would never do. The farmer let them picnic in his meadow with the stream flowing through the middle. Wildflowers grew there. They could pick them, he said, but they must shut the gates, because of cattle straying. He didn't feel obliged to allow them, but their mother paid good rent. Playing in his meadow was a privilege. He and his wife felt pity for the mother, good doctor woman, left with two.

So the girls paddled in his brook in summer and hid away under his footbridge, where Village eyes could not see. They waded in water floating with weeds, ranunculus, crowfoot and dissolving cowdung. Their toes contacted tin cans. They looked at hoof-marks in mud where kingcups grew. They were pestered by horseflies. Mosquitoes clustered under the bridge where lumps of dung adhered to the stonework. They often went. Until the day the thundering hooves went over them. They'd heard, standing in the water, cold with fear. Joanna wet herself. 'It's cavalry' she said. With spurs and orange teeth. A minotaur perhaps. They would be killed. Hope said that it was knights. With shields and penants, riding to crusade. Their mother had been vexed. 'Don't be so fanciful. The farmer owns no horses and half a dozen cows, some of which are due to calve. Joanna

37

is too inventive. Wetting at her age is dirty.' Their bites had turned
septic. They were told not to go near the brook, to eat their marmite
sandwiches under an oak tree. Why not pick flowers, make a cowslip
ball? They went on paddling, but not near the bridge. They picked
cow parsley, collected spawn in jam jars to hide in mud holes, running
in the evening air to rid their clothes of dung smells. They collected
cuckoo spit on their fingers, to show their mother; proof of an
interest in botany. They talked about their fears in the meadow as
they splashed their feet. Fears of ghosts, fears of sudden noises,
Village kids, fears of their father when he came to visit them. Fears of
their mother's smile 'He's coming to see you today. Won't that be
lovely? You'll have a splendid time.' They knew that she dreaded it
more than they, hiding upstairs when he arrived. The farmer's wife
let him in. The farmer's wife was avid for detail. The city gent with
car who came to take the little things to lunch in a hotel. He stuffed
them unsuitably, and they used to farmfresh fare and her baking.
Both girls vomited after avocado pears. Then their mother said 'We
won't be seeing him so often, he's going to marry another lady. As
soon as it's made absolute.' That meant she could put away his
photograph and forget him. A relief not to have to smile and prepare
for hiding when he came. About that time Joanna started sleep-
walking. The farmer and his wife thought the mother brave and
devoted, a pleasure to let rooms to. The town doctor-lady and her
girls, staying on the farm until they got their lives in order were
remembered in the Village.

They moved to London, to the redbrick house in Putney. At first
their mother tried to housekeep like the farmer's wife, to bake them
doughnuts for their tea, to cook boiled bacon on the bone. Cooking
bored her. The business crystallized before their first London
Christmas. 'We'll have a real feast, a beano,' she had said. A feast of
her own making and never mind the man who'd left them. She'd
made the room look jolly with tinsel and awful painted leaves, had
started to make the cake while they were sleeping. They would be
merry, just the three. Half sloshed on sherry, she had measured,
chopped, peeled the ingredients listed by Better Cakes. Such
quantity, such grating, slicing fuss was out of all proportion. She'd put
aside the board and knife, had stuffed her mouth with candied peel to
grind and bite, chewing with her teeth and tongue before spitting into

38

the colander, rinsing the pieces free of spit and sherry. She'd sensed the eyes of the elder girl, whose name she temporarily forgot. She'd known then, that housekeeping was not her role, that birth-control advising was. 'Don't eat the cake Joanna, it's full of *her* saliva' Hope had said. So it had been chucked out, brown, damp, failed, another witness to a failed marriage. Post-Christmas snow had lain for weeks, the bins got overstuffed, the cake stared like a reproach. A flop. The girls went down with flu. Tending them with milky slops she felt they were repellent, bad blood that should have flowed away, instead of forming into creatures, not quite twins. Decided then to make it her life's work to prevent birth, to take a course and specialise, to put away the sherry. She'd bought hornrims, bought a set of kitchen mops, become methodical. She chose a high-powered vacuum, with attachments to poke into ceiling corners. She sprinkled bleach round germy areas. Her desk was tidy, managerial. Grief for a relationship that failed changed to pride in her professional role. Her state of singleness was pleasant. Her own bed at night, and peace. Six years later, habit and routine were second nature. She worked long hours, kept downstairs at home as antiseptic as her surgery. She paid bills quickly. The letterbox was refilled daily with sample creams, the latest rubber appliance and pills. If she had a weakness it was for houseplants of the hardy kind. Their slow growth was a reward. Such plants were an example of right living, staying in one place, multiplying minimally. She loved her cacti, they demanded no attention. She controlled them. They didn't whisper behind her back, lock themselves away like druids over rites or leave the fur of animals behind them. They didn't bang doors in her face, they simply produced prickles. Sometimes she talked into their spines. 'If it were not for my work, I'd give up, resign. Bringing up those sluts is no picnic I can tell you. My love, you've budded. Watch it.' Evening lecturing was another escape from the sluts. Her ex-husband's offer of the house in London in lieu of further maintenance was well timed. Work had been her cure. Only she'd never dreamed her girls would turn against her, despise her for her labours that kept them in idleness. They watched with malice-sharpened eyes, demanded fresh extras. She earned the means to get them tennis racquets, fruit and music for that Hoaley place. They never smiled or thanked her. Something was missing in the home. It couldn't be the presence of their faithless father. Through no fault of hers the home lacked devotion. She couldn't comprehend them. At work, her teenage patients loved her. They came to her in suppliance. Their tears were rending. Their periods were late, don't let it happen, don't confirm the dreaded. Please, what to do to avoid another? Please, these circumstances qualify for abortion. Please, are there ways of making husbands cooler? They looked at her with gratitude. They didn't give her lip, they gave her cash. 'Oh cactus, do not bud', she said again.

Circulars addressed to Hope arrived through the post. She'd written off for information about camping grounds, riding stables, holiday resorts because she felt restless. She hung about the hall each morning, to snatch her envelopes away from her mother's post.

'If you don't show me', said Joanna, 'I'll tell about that awful gypsy person. You've been going to his boiler room again. You've got letters on your brain. Show me.'

Hope didn't speak and hid the letters in her bag. She showed the Continental ones to Lavender. It was the summer of embroidered bags. Hope and Lavender dictated what the school should wear. Their hair, makeup and slang were studied. Eye-makeup in small pots were carried round with text books to make faces look like tropical birds. Felt-tipped pens in brilliant colours were in vogue because of Hope. She turned vegetarian. Ham provided by their mother turned hard and red in its bed of lettuce. 'They reject my groceries, that's the latest. They treat me like poison' she whispered to her cacti and cursed again the man who had encumbered her, running off to Florida with another.

Joanna wished for a different life. A life with a mother like Miss Delicate and a sister who loved and depended on her. The cactus plants embodied all that was uncomfortably painful and wrong in the Putney home. She listened to Lavender telling of her home. The Chargers were tolerant of adolescent whims. The mother continued to plunge thermometers into roasting joints, to pour cream on Sunday puddings regardless of tempers, and she was always there. The home dissent in Putney was because of their mother's work. Because of it they were at loggerheads and led three separate lives, the secret signs of which stayed hidden in their desks and bags. She couldn't bear not reading what Hope hid away. Hope was a two-faced beast.

40

Mallory was an early riser. He liked to read the Daily Mirror, for betting information mostly. The Major liked a little bet as well. They swapped tips and were collaborators, though Mallory despised a person of the Major's ability, who had to end his days tutoring on the cheap, with nothing put aside for rainy days. Mallory would better himself. That was why he liked to help with the classes, it wasn't only to put the young ladies through their prances, it was a chance to learn, to read their exercises. His uncles taught him to write a lovely hand, as well as make things. He liked embellishment, liked notes to look nice. Something to do with handwriting or horses would be his ideal career. He was adept at figures too, because of totting odds. There were opportunities for advancement in his work at Hoaley. After looking at his Mirror, making a note of what looked tempting he checked the roller towels in the Cloaks, to let them stay another day where possible. He mopped corridors, turned the date over on Miss Delicate's heavy wooden calender. Toilet cleaning might not be highly regarded but he was proud of doing everything well. To be appreciated meant a lot to him. He was Miss D.'s right arm. He copied down sentiments from the blackboard, poetry or a thought from the brain of Miss Delicate herself. His taste was for the romantic. 'When I am dead, my dearest, Sing no sad songs for me; Plant thou no roses at my head, Nor shady cypress tree.' Hope Greenham was more than dearest, she was his darlingest. He dreamed of Lady Right. Since seeing Hope he thought he'd found her. No wonder he was grateful to Miss Delicate and Hoaley, his waiting was worthwhile, he'd spotted Hope, his darlingest, and yearned. She had the breeding that he looked for, a delicacy and a little hint of naughtiness. And virgin. He went over points as he squeezed old bits of soap into a wire container. He'd bridle her, touch and mould her to his liking. He gave a great rubbing to the end mirror, where she soon would be standing. He wasn't such a bad looker himself, his summer tan was youthifying. He'd risk his neck for her.

Lavender was first in. 'My brother and I have christian-named our parents for years. My dears, believe it if you can, when tots we called them Moth and Feather.'

'But Lav., how sweet.'

"Sweet", she says. Under no circs would I sanction marriage. Your lot are divorced aren't they Hope?'

41

'But Lav. if there are babies? Children should have some security don't you agree?'

'Oh balls. The nuclear family is dead. As dead as war and beer. The Group must assume the onus. The Group is the alternative.'

'I agree about war. War must cease. I don't care for violence.' Violence took place in the newspapers that she and Joanna threw away. Drink was for putting into cakes you threw away. Lavender was a bag of wind.

' "Must cease", she says. A change is on the way. You'll see. A bloodless revolution.' Lavender was at her most earnest, flicking spit out with her words. Pot should be universally available. Down with authority. She wore huge metal-framed specs. Her tongue filled the space between her teeth like a third round lens.

'Now, Ladies, please. Enlightenment. The bell is about to peal.'

Hope reached into her shoe-bag. Increasingly it seemed, her fingers lived in order to touch notes. Her nails, like painted eyes, spotted envelopes and signalled to her. 'Another letter. What a lark.' She was possessed by Mallory, she lived to feel his hands on her. True love had come at last. Her fingers quivered.

At times Miss Delicate became afflicted with a kind of transport, swaying in front of her girls and babbling. Euphemia began to squirm, their lady looked so queer. Their Head was off her nut. Miss Delicate knew she should stop it, these spells attacked her when she sensed mischief. Young Hope was up to something that she couldn't put her finger on. The air felt uneasy. She blessed her dependable Mallory. Her staff might be past their prime but he was A1. 'We give thanks to the fates that govern our destiny, for water for swimming, for soap and holly berries. Our daily rice, a sharpened pencil and healthy limbs to dance our alphabet, for Maths, for French and tennis Ooooh.'

The hall was filled with restless nudging and fidgetting. The Delly was overdoing things with a vengeance.

'Hope, I say Hope. You got another letter. I saw you at your shoebag. Show me. Show me or I'll tell.'

'Shut up you ape.'

'You must let me look at it. You've got to.'

'Once and for all get out of my life. I never wish to see your face. Drop dead.'

'Ooooh. Give thanks for the moon, the wind under our hooves, for those in orbit Ooooh.'

The Major and Madame looked worried. These signs were dangerous. Miss Delicate was astray, their jobs might be at risk.

4

The letter Miss Delicate held was so shocking she felt ready for the sick list. She had been right to sense trouble, delaying the conclusion of her protracted prayers. She had taken the letter from Joanna with a sense of doom. Rarely were letters happy things; bills, complaints, requests for something inconvenient were her lot. She'd never had a love letter. Time had now put paid to that hope. But love should be enobling. 'My Hope of the World. Come to the boiler-room for you know what. Signed from yours E.M.'

In all her years of teaching she'd never felt so shattered. She leaned back, looking for courage at the blindfold girl in the picture by G.F. Watts, twanging her broken-stringed lute. Her light had gone out. Signed from yours E.M. That jack-in-office steward had stretched a hand, had settled his eye on Hope, had written a note that reduced love to sewerage. Love was about to be desecrated on her premises.

Her breathing became heavy as she made up her mind. She wouldn't flinch. She lumbered down the path, past yellow flowers that stained her sensible stockings, brushing the rake entwined with convolvulus. She opened the door: one look was enough. Her star prospect was being lewd with the care-taker. Like Pandora opening the box she had come upon wickedness. She looked and they looked back. Mallory had a particularly unpleasant look about the mouth, she'd seen that look on the face of an animal trainer, years ago, prodding wild beasts in a ring.

She shut the door, walked back, forcing her breathing to the count of four. This was her Armageddon. This was worse than Lavender walking the guttering, worse than Euphemia being sick into the piano, worse than the feminine towel hung over the clock hands. This was worse than dementia praecox. She hadn't had a flush in years, was threatened with one now. Her dress became soaked around the waist. She dabbed her brow and upper lip with blotting paper, she fanned herself with Lavender's essay on the behaviour of mammals.

The two had been indulging in carnality. Mallory's hand had been put upon a portion of Hope's anatomy. He must be fired. Hope must be asked to leave.

'I am a Baptist', he had said, 'and not afraid of work.' Had settled for a less than average wage. He'd told her that he liked a position with scope for versatility. She hadn't asked which school he knew, she hadn't checked his references, and all to save a stamp. Too late now, his colour showed. He'd trifled with Hope, their two white faces gaped through thick smoke, caught out. Had it been Hope who hung the towel over the clock hands at noon? Would Joanna be contaminated too? Too late to bewail her lack of funds. The mischief was done, the rumpus couldn't be avoided. Lack of a stamp had been her downfall. Lack of cash prevented her from hiring people suitable to man her school. Lack of cash forced her to make do with shabby tools, a broken building, rice-based food and very old clothes. She taught subjects for which she had no skill; her classes wouldn't stand inspection. The irony of it, when all she wanted was to paint, to dance her alphabeticals and scrape a tune. Hope had broken trust, she was a demon.

'Call Hope Greenham' she shouted at Euphemia Draye.

'Well, Hope, Explanations will not help you. Your mother will receive a letter. Go to the remedial room, stay there until four.'

'Explanation, Miss Delicate? What explanation? We were only playing about. Just fooling.'

'You call that playing? Sport? There is no place here Hope. No place at Hoaley for you.'

'But really, please, it wasn't serious. I mean, I suppose it did look funny and I'm sorry.' She didn't want their mother getting fraught letters, she hadn't bargained for that. Hope looked at Miss Delicate with her artless open-eyed face. 'Really Miss Delicate, I promise you.'

'Go', repeated Miss Delicate.

The remedial room was curtainless, a room for those who were unwell. It was bare except for a couch and books to look at. 'Fear not Flappers', 'Attic Attitudes' by Gertrude V. Delicate, published at her own expense long ago. She passed Madame who asked 'You're feeling indisposed, Hope? Don't fly, child.'

Miss Delicate filled her fat green pen. She scarcely knew if she were male or female. The girl must need a brain surgeon.

'Dear Dr. Greenham, I feel it my bounden duty to ask you to withdraw your daughter from Hoaley. Her conduct forces me to take his measure. We at Hoaley aim to foster Art, a love of Fine Things. She has been Unfine. We stand for decency, we do not countenance lechery.' She crossed this out, re-writing 'debauchery' over-writing again 'lewdness'. The result was messy. She felt too ill to start again. She signed it with a rush, Gertrude V. Delicate.

The letter eased her system, like a serpent who had bitten she felt less venomous. To her life's end she wouldn't forget the stare from Hope's blue eyes. Next, Mallory.

She'd put the note in his pay packet, leave it in the room above the boiler house. She let him have this place for a pound a week. Here he could take his recreation, eat his lunch or do accounts to help her. His balancing of books had been invaluable, he had the knack of making figures match. The problem of his replacement was a serious one. She couldn't take on any more herself, today's events proved that. Today she felt her age. Madame already did too much, helping Major, tennis-coaching as well as all that French. Perhaps, if rightly handled, Madame might be coaxed into tending the boiler, might even welcome the chance to be of further use in her delightful Frenchy way. Good lady, another of life's casualties, orphaned at forty, pre-occupied with the perils of flying, she might positively benefit by having more to do.

Geography must wait. 'Get them singing', she told Euphemia. 'Sing "Boatman do not Tarry" until I get back.' She'd serve the knave his writ before acquainting the girls any further with trade winds. She thought again how many small dark rooms the building had. The pantry where poor Geld concocted his rice mixtures for dinner was little more than a cubby hole. By making everyone do the work of two she could run the school with four adults and poor Geld. The staff were jacks and jills of all trades. A corner of her heart wept as she tried humming 'Boatman do not Tarry, and I'll give thee a Silver Pound'.

A flight of outside stairs led to Mallory's office over the boiler room. Broken flowerpots, racquets needing strings and flower pots were on the steps. Nothing was thrown out. Like William Morris Miss Delicate believed in owning nothing that wasn't useful as well as beautiful. Mallory had been unbeautiful. He had been foul.

A thump from her knuckles opened his door. She'd caught him changing. The swinging door surprised him, he missed his footing, tripping against the leg of his trousers and almost knocked her down. As he straightened she saw something peeping from the slit of his pants, something like a miniature trunk, something mauve and rude. The rude animal appendage of a rude animal person. A fine person would keep it hidden, decently buttoned at all times or else concealed beneath a fig-leaf. She almost shouted 'Fire', 'Ladies please'. It was an offence.

'You're fired sir. Leave at once. Fired. You hear me?'

'What, now this minute? Hold on now, old girl. Easy with the baby.'

'I beg your pardon? Fired is what I said. Please leave.' She prayed for a platoon of policemen, the law, with truncheons and navy serge that buttoned over their unspeakable parts, she prayed for firemen. Thank the fates she was a spinster with no knowledge of such trunks. Such hair all coarse and curly, twining round its base, was something she'd stay unfamiliar with.

'Now easy. That ain't . . . isn't legal Miss. What's up then?'

'Get out. Go. Pack your bags', Miss Delicate repeated. His pretended innocence, the way he leered was horrid.

'Your trouble is you've never seen a dick. A dick is something you ain't seen. Take a look then.'

'Oooh . . . ' She was afraid she'd fall down.

'Oooh' he mimicked. 'Know it again now?'

'Leave', she moaned.

'Don't you worry Miss. I'm leaving. You didn't need to bother. I'm off.' Breeze off right now and thanks for the memory. He'd got the message, got wind of her temper. Quit the premises before things got too hot. He'd gone too far, should not have insulted her. Regretted it already, but she asked for it. The pity was he admired good manners, rated manners highly and admired Miss Delicate's aims. He felt like crying really. He loved the lovely girl with yellow hair. He'd stretched a hand out to the moon, the moon had reached back. He'd told her that he loved her, there behind his boiler. It wouldn't be the end. He'd get in touch.

'Be out within the hour' Miss Delicate said. She saw his case containing neatly arranged clothes. His shoes were laid out ready to be packed. There was a pile of Mirrors, a pencil and a cheap box camera. Mad-man. Lecher. A good thing that she provided no bed for him. She'd let him have an old armchair, a wooden stool to put his feet up. 'A quiet room, make use of it', she'd told him at the interview. And docked a pound each week. The room would soon be vacant. There would be no trace here of her handiman, her Baptist, who was not afraid of work, and who she'd never see again.

She left him. It was over. The mother whose child had been struck by a brainstorm would get the letter next day. One less pupil, depleted staff. Old and fuddled, she seized up a tureen of rice from poor Geld.

'Ladies please, luncheon is served. Lavender, Euphemia, Joanna put up the trestles for the meal. Do not tarry.'

By spooning rice onto plates and bustling she tried to forget the girl's blue stare, his laugh and his appendage. She appealed to her spirit guides, her Isadora, Rosetti, Hunt, the fine people who put their work first and whose amorous peccadilloes were merely interestingly quaint. Procreation should be left in the hands of artists, preferably married, whose work was testimony rather than their children. Her mission was to guide her girls to knowledge. How they got into the world was of no concern. How parents set about the business, what went into where she'd never quite discovered.

Hope saw Mallory from the remedial room. He held his case under his arm, his shoulders looked miserable. His face was full of regrets until he saw her. He smiled up at her window and beckoned.

Madame and Major guessed what had happened and they guessed the consequence. Extra work all round. Major preened his moustache having swallowed down some rice. He'd lost a tipster and a friend. His working days would be colourless. He didn't care to give up more time to Hoaley, time that could be spent more interestingly on the turf. Madame fetched a fly-spray and gunned them down as they flew, her mouse face resolute. Some girls complained that flies fell in their food. Some of them brought cheese and dates to help the dinner down, they flicked the stones about and spun the knives to see who would get married, who'd be rich. Euphemia showed some of her doggerel to Joanna, seizing the chance. Joanna would be a goner now.

Miss Delicate's letter arrived at the home in Putney before their mother left. 'Is the lady responsible for herself? The letter is unintelligible.'

'What letter is it?' Joanna asked.

'From Miss Delicate. Has one of you been lewd? Which is it? There, read it. One of you has been ordered out for debauching on premises. Really, how extreme.'

'It's me', Hope said. 'She means me. The woman is off her rocker. She says that I'm expelled.'

'It all seems somewhat hasty. You made enough fuss to get into the school. And next term's fees are paid. What went wrong, may I ask?' All those pipe lessons, laburnum trees, eurythmics and heaven knew what. It was inconsiderate. She hardly blamed the woman for not naming the girl. She tended to get them confused herself. Their similarity was misleading, but it was bungling of Miss Delicate to allow debauching on the site. Now Hope had no school to go to, would be cooling her heels all day. Hoaley was convenient, though what they learned there she'd yet to see. An alternative school would have to be located, just when her work programme was over-full. The two would be separated. They were too much alone already, when split up they'd by isolated. One girl sang quite sweetly, she believed.

'Do you want to go on being educated, Hope? There's more to life than making sweets and dreaming.'

'I want to leave.'

'You're sure? That's settled. Joanna, you had better stay. I've paid, after all. During the summer we will think. Decide on something for you both. Settle the future.'

'That would be best', Hope said, staring at her mother's dark hair, and the few grey hairs at the temple. It was impossible to think of her loving. She could never have run recklessly to meet a lover, yet she had recourse to a tin marked 'Self'.

'Is that the time? I'm late.' What mattered was to reach her surgery on time, to greet the patients with her mind uncluttered by expulsions or lewdness on school premises. Perhaps she could still get a refund from the mad woman. It was an object lesson. These sluts were proof of what could happen. A warning. She must redouble her efforts to ensure that others stayed free of the trap. Stayed free of the boredom, the physical toll, the loss of identity, the limitation of outlook that resulted from childbirth. Populations mustn't be allowed to explode, she'd see to it personally. She assumed that the expelled one had been prudent, prepared herself. They had no need of indoctrination, though what the two of them thought about she'd no inkling. They hung about, lacking purpose, nothing to show at the end of their day but a pile of dishes and animal fur on their clothing. Random conception was ultimate improbity, she'd paid the price herself. Suppression of birth was her *raison d'être*. Sluts.

'What will you do now, Hope?' Joanna asked. She was sad. She'd watched Miss Delicate with her bowl of rice, condoled in silence with her. Sympathy could only express itself by repeatedly helping herself to undercooked rice. She couldn't comfort her, could only eat until she nearly puked. She too had seen Mallory with his case before he waved to Hope. She had been glad. Let him go. Now she and Hope could be together, like before.

'I'm going back to bed'. Hope said.

'I can't face school alone. What about the tournament?' She'd been looking forward to reading Hope's name on the gilt cup standing on a shelf in the hall. She was afraid of the eyes of the girls in the Cloaks. They'd want to know the details, like greedy birds tearing at food.

'I'm scarcely interested in tennis playing. That school is like a tomb, like being buried alive.'

'You chose it. You used to quite like it, Hope.'

'People change, they grow. I'm going back to sleep.' She tipped Miss Delicate's letter from the table, enjoying stepping on it. She took some walnuts from a bowl. Hope could crack walnuts with her teeth, scattering the shells. Her future stretched, leisured, eating health food, playing chopsticks. She could visit the planetarium or take a Turkish bath. She said leave the breakfast dishes to her, knowing that the table would stay uncleared, with marmalade smearing the bread knife, egg yolk on the cup-handles. She went upstairs. The rabbit would roam freely now.

Joanna did her teeth. The bathroom stayed immaculate. Their mother had polished the bath that morning; the mirror smelled of methylated.

Hope's quilt billowed over her ears. She lay with her back to the door, her bare skin showing pink against the violet cotton. The down on each vertebrae was highlighted in the sun, the flat bones of her shoulder blades were like triangles. One foot stuck out, shells still

50

adhering to the sole. Her back alone had style, though her yellow hair was hidden. Her hairbrush lay on her piano keys, the bristles powdered with Turkish Delight from a box that Mallory had given her. The string horse stood near the sweets on dainty hooves. Also on the keys were pots of make-up, rouge and coloured creams that had gone hard from exposure to the air. Once she had the girls following her lead she turned to something else. She had planned to get her wrists tattooed with hearts and horses. Hoaley girls would miss her leadership. Lavender lacked her inventiveness though she was more brave and cruel.

'What shall I say? Miss Delicate will expect you there today. We haven't broken up.'

'Just say I've gone into orbit. Now bugger off.'

'What will you do next?'

'Mind your own business.'

'But tell me.'

'I may go to the coast. I might.' Hope's voice was thick from sleepiness and the violet quilt.

'The coast? What coast. You've been getting circulars. Has he been writing to you. What have you arranged? Oh Hope, you won't run off?'

'Why not? I might.'

'You can't. It isn't love.'

'Love? What's love to do with it?' Hope pulled back the quilt. Joanna was a romantic. Joanna's mind was mazed with movies. Vows, arum lilies, hanging over tiny heads in cots. 'Be mine', 'You have my heart'. Love was a trick. She wasn't going to end up like their mother, loving in order to be rejected. Their mother's so-called love, her tin marked 'Self' had helped no-one. She'd loved and been let down, been stuck with two children because the Courts decreed. Love boiled down to care and custody. A child's views were not considered. Their mother didn't care that she had been expelled in ignominy, she only cared about her sacred time. 'Anyway, Mallory says he adores me. Does that please you?'

'Wait, Hope, it's not the real thing. The real thing will come. You mustn't compromise.'

'I'll find out if it's real by testing it. Life is a compromise', Hope said grandly. It pleased her when he said he loved her. He said he always

51

would, whispering the lovely words in the smoke before he went away for good. She'd sneaked down from the Remedial room for the goodbye. He said he'd send a postcard, that they were made for each other, she was just to wait. He'd keep her posted.

'What coast do you mean?' Joanna imagined Hope hanging over prows of speed boats, winning beauty competitions by bathing pools wearing spikey heels. Blurred pictures of Hope at Hoaley would appear on breakfast tables. 'Have you seen this girl?' 'Mystery of vanishing Hope'. The press would bang at the Putney door for information.

'You shadow me as if we were Siamese twins. I have an independent life. Now bugger off.' Her plan was clear. Hope had a knack of falling instantly to sleep. Sleep came like medicine, erasing tiredness and excitement. Sleep took away guilt, the guilt of hurting Jo. She wanted to forget the look on Joanna's face.

Joanna left. She was afraid of school without her, afraid Hope would forget her.

5

'I'm going to miss Hope dreadfully', Lavender said. She was unchallenged now. Her frizzy hair was arranged into a kind of crown and her tongue pushed words wetly into Joanna's face. Joanna wiped a fleck off her cheek. 'You must be lost Jo. Do you miss her?'

'I do a bit.'

'Poor little Jojo missed big sister a bit. Hilarious. Where is Mallory?'

'I don't know.'

'What did your mother say? What will Hope do?'

'Our mother believes in letting us decide. I shall probably leave myself.'

'I didn't credit Hope with so much guile. Come to the Remedial room at break. I have another book. Danish.'

'I have a note for Miss Delicate.'

'We mustn't forget dear teacher. Still writing "I love you" messages?'

Joanna's time at school wasn't spent yearning for Miss Delicate but worrying about whether Hope would be there when she got home. Thinking about the home without her made her feel ill. Though their old closeness hadn't been resumed. The school was under strain as well, the staff were tired. Alphabetical posturing was cancelled. Major organised maintenance parties. Once he had them all sweeping, stoking, tidying, he sneaked off to listen to his transistor. He missed his guide and mentor.

Miss Delicate had suggested to Dr. Greenham that Joanna might take cookery lessons. Girls would bring their own ingredients, dishes handed round later at lunch. It was not, alas, her wont to return a pupil's fees, once term had started. She polished the challenge cup on which Hope's name wouldn't appear and felt afraid that Joanna would follow in her sister's steps. The summer would be warm, she'd save on coke. In August she would come herself to labour with nails and paint, take pride in navigating her own craft. 'Boatman do not Tarry', she hummed, her lips set in a line.

'The woman is mean as well as mad', Dr. Greenham said when she read about the extra cookery.

Each day Hope lay in bed. Apart from collecting weeds for the rabbit she did nothing. Her quilt was scattered with chewed leaves. She watched the post. Joanna was not invited in. She stood in the bedroom doorway after school looking at Hope reading with the rabbit. She didn't play her piano and was not interested to hear that Lavender missed her. Lavender asked to see Joanna's poems because she fancied becoming a poet herself, an Underground one of course.

Miss Delicate asked Joanna to return her sister's books, not saying Hope's name. The girl had been lewd. Fine art and fine action were synonymous. She planned a talk on the theme as she ripped clean pages out for scrap. She ruled the elder Greenham girl's name out with red ink, writing D.D. for dishonourable discharge in her register. She hoped the fates would be kind, that Mallory would be forgotten soon, and gossip would die down. Lavender's limbs got browner, her hair frizzier. Her spitty tongue appeared to widen.

A postcard from the coast arrived among their mother's samples in the letterbox. On the back of a picture of a merry-go-round Mallory wrote 'Be at Victoria on Saturday twelve-thirty ready for a spell by the sea with me your escort. Signed from yours E.M.' Joanna read it, knowing then the feel of real jealousy. It marked Hope's entry into adulthood. She knew Hope would hide it in her knicker drawer with the letter from the St. Ives boy and the hanky of their father's used as a bit on the only occasion Hope had ridden a horse. He'd fixed his hanky in the horse's mouth and guided her. 'Don't pull so hard', he'd said. The horse belonged to the lady, now his wife, in Florida. She lent her belt to fix onto the hanky. 'Don't pull so hard.' The lady loved her horses, owned a stables, taught children as a sideline. There was mutual distrust between the sisters and her, but the hanky stayed a relic, stiff-dried, smelling as though their father had blown his nose on it.

Hope was happy for Joanna to look at the postcard. Now things were made plain. Soon she'd be leaving Joanna for good, she was making an escape. 'I'm not disappearing to outer space. It's only the South coast.'

'You can't. You mustn't. I beg you, think again.' It wasn't only that her world revolved round her, Hope was so ill-prepared for running. She only had two pounds ten.

'Oh stop moaning. Kill-joy. I'm relying on you to look after the rabbit.'

'Don't I always?'

Tying its paws with towels, poking the nozzle into the rage-flattened ears had been their last shared occupation. Its red eyes looked insane as it grunted. 'You ought to take some food at least. It's all so uncertain, Hope.'

'I'll send for anything I need. I'm dying to see what the place is like. I can't wait.'

'You should pack clothes. Do be careful.' She wanted to tell Hope to go on loving her, not to forget, to go on needing her. 'Do take care.'

'Oh shut up. Look after his ears. I'll write.'

'Goodbye, goodbye', Joanna waved the towel from which the white fur fell. The dreaded thing had happened, Hope had gone. Waiting for it was the worst. She knew now where she stood: there was nothing to look forward to except loneliness and envy. Outside the kitchen window by the letterbox she saw the dog rolling again. The house was dead.

Hope felt unreal, as though part of her skull had been removed. This was how people must feel before committing hari-kiri. Her skirt trailed in the dust by the bus stop. She'd aimed at a wild loose look, buffing her cheeks to give them a shine and wearing her hair bedraggled. She hummed nervously as she got on the bus. 'Victoria' she said to the conductor who answered 'Oh, your Majesty' She knew that he would remember her and think about her through the day. A fare like her, lemon-smelling, raffish-looking was rare on his route. A lemony girl in a long green skirt.

There was no Mallory in the station arcade, only a crowd of trippers who stared at her because she was so different. They felt suspicious of a tall, long-skirted girl with a nosebag on her shoulder. She was upper-class and had no luggage. She knew she was looking at her best. Heat suited her, brought out her beauty, like sun on fruit. Mallory should be there. He had a nerve. She liked the people watching her, speculatively. She heard them murmur. 'Bit of a higher stepper!' 'Tart, more like.' 'She did ought to wear more clothes,

55

showing everything and how's your father.' 'Long-distance lorry girl. Isn't wearing pants.' She looked at some pigeons pecking on the platform while people milled round the arrival indicator board. A small boy ran at the pigeons who left the ground reluctantly.

'Leave off bloody teasing, Herb. Leave that or we'll miss us train.' The boy's mother was so fat that moving was uncomfortable. She envied Hope her thinness and wondered why she stared at birds like that, dreaming her life away. She envied her her freedom from a crowd of kids.

Hope watched the birds' neat red feet picking daintily among the litter. Pigeons fascinated her, and gulls. Ruthless, they knew how to survive by making use of humans. She wished her nosebag contained more than two pounds ten and her hairbrush of best hog's bristle. She looked round again and spotted Mallory watching by the arriving taxis.

His face in profile looked wretched. He clenched and unclenched his fists and his eyelids were withered with the worry of missing her entirely. He'd posted her the card on a tide of joy, having recovered from the humiliation of his dismissal once he got away from London. After leaving Hope he'd made for the coast, his case under his arm. He'd worked on holiday camps, knew he'd find employment. This camp provided work of all categories. He'd signed on pronto. The sea air suited him, it was rejuvenating. He'd grown his hair a little longer, he felt he compared well with any youngster. Folk came from all parts to the camp; as good as foreign travel. Rover he was and rover he'd remain but he couldn't get the Hoaley girl out of his memory. Sending for her was a risk.

'You came', he said, face smoothing with relief.

'I've been here hours. You ought to get glasses.'

'I thought you'd come by taxi.' He wouldn't admit to short sight, though faces tended to blurr now, seen from any distance. He stood up straight. He'd forgotten how tall Hope was. He put his hand into his pocket, like an executive. Then he remembered that they hadn't kissed. He leaned over clumsily to touch her hair.

'Is our train in?' She was put off by his suit of hairy tweed. She missed his screwdrivers and his school shoes with the squashy soles. In the dull station light her lover showed up timidly. An ill-at-ease man in a cow-coloured suit with pointy shoes. He kept his fingers curled with shyness. He kept glancing away as though afraid to look at her. 'Haven't you got no . . . any luggage? Where are your cases?' he asked. If that contraption on her shoulder was all that she had the girl was in for a cold. No wonder he hadn't recognised her. Her school dresses were short enough in all conscience, but in that trailing get-up she looked almost loose. He'd sooner have her in her stripey dress. The coast was cool, what with sea breezes and that, and here she was improperly attired. In Victoria Station his moongirl looked a twopenny thing. Her manner, too, had changed, not looking at him with eyes of love, her eyes seemed more interested in a set of pigeons. He'd always hated pigeons, dirty things, messing, doing damage, scavenging. He wasn't keen on birds at all.

'I like to feel free, not to be tied down', she said. The pigeons pecking made her think of Joanna who had begged her with a desperate face to eat before she left. The toast had burned under the grill while she implored her. Now she felt empty. There was a smell of sweetened tea in the station.

'We must make sure of our places. You have to look sharp or you don't get seats.' He was eager to be practical, to be in charge. If he had his way he'd poison birds, all flying things. They must get on the train. He took her arm. Touching made you more relaxed. They'd get back their old footing once alone.

She said she wanted something to eat but he drew her to the waiting train. The trippers were beginning to push, using their cardboard cases as battering rams against each other's legs and swearing. Hold-alls burst their zips from the strain of carrying bright holiday clothing. Getting started on holiday was a sweat. You had to push to get a seat in the Pullmans. 'Come on Herb. Hurry, you little bugger, get into the Pullman.' The fat mother flopped into a corner, her children round her.

Mallory explained that he had the morning off to fetch her. He got a window seat for her opposite some midget men whose feet dangled as they sat. The two had had to jump to reach the seat and now they sat with calm expressions. People gave them preference because of their size. When on holiday, instead of getting kicked to death they got consideration, so they smiled. The London children and their brother Herb liked watching them. They found the little gents as good as anything in Bertram Mills, they delighted in their tiny tailored clothes and buckled shoes.

'A pity it's so packed. I'll stand by you', said Mallory. His face warmed because those small chaps affronted him. He wished he'd stopped further up the platform. They were creepy. Like pigeons the grossly handicapped should be painlessly exterminated. They stared at Hope as if they had the witch's eye. He wanted to give Hope the holiday of her life, he hadn't reckoned on such a noisy crowd or being thrown in with dwarves. As for those fat children, they were pests, digging each other with lolly sticks and bright green fishing nets. Cases filled the aisles. The carriage was bursting.

Hope and the little gents were the only cool and smiling people. They sensed each other's superior merit, the three of them had a bond, they drew attention. People stared at Hope for her beauty and the gents for their deformity.

The fat mother raised one hand to pop peanuts to her mouth, laying out against her fat kids with the other. The jaws of all the family moved round cheese sandwiches. From now until they got back home in a week's time their mouths wouldn't be empty. As the train slipped away from the platform the people settled to the serious rustling of bags and boxes containing food. The less ravenous ones chewed gum, or contented themselves with smoking behind their papers, though there was barely room to open these, they had to fold them sitting sideways. It was better to munch some little titbit. The fat mother explained that she made sure to bring rations. Travelling was tiring, a spot of grub helped. Hope looked at the sandwiches. Mallory looked out of the window, feeling grumpy. Standing was a bind. Their meetings at Hoaley had been occupied in the acquaintance of their bodies. It was time they talked. He'd counted on a talk while travelling down, a talk in a quiet corner out of earshot where their minds could meet. He lit a cigarette. The slummy view was nothing to shout about, a succession of ancient blackened buildings slung with washing and yards containing used tyres. Grit blew in. Their engine drowned the noise from hooters or chimes from steeple clocks and no-one cared but him. The trippers didn't notice heat or dirt or sweat, the discomfort of tight clothes, they had their eatables and smokes, their week had started now. Standing with cases denting your calves was bloody.

'Have a ciggy, Hope dear?'

'What? I don't smoke thank you. I never have. I didn't know you did.' So his smokey smell at school had been cigarettes as well as the boiler. He told her that he'd smoked for many years, had tried to pack it in, but failed. Hope said that it was revolting, her voice ringing clearly round the carriage. She sounded censorious, the trippers looked wary. Was she criticising, the stuck-up cow? The gents nodded their curly heads in agreement. They knew the dangers of a cigarette, they never did except for a cigar on their birthday. Smoking sapped the health and stained the fingernails. They prided themselves on health, their smart appearance. Fitness was a duty. The fat mother opened an eye in Hope's direction. Silly bitch. A person had to die, cancer, overweight, too many kids, it didn't make no difference. Her fat children sniggered over the edges of sandwiches, all of them smokers of long standing. Mallory rubbed the butt against his pointy shoe and said he wished he was able to abstain, he simply couldn't. Hope smiled and said he ought to try again, for her, and could she have some food? The sight of all those munching mouths made her feel faint. Those not eating something sucked straws stuck into cans. The leader of the little gents, the one with the larger head, took out a picnic basket. Serviettes were folded in the lid, the cups were doll-sized. 'Please be our guest, we bake our own confectionery. These fairy cakes were prepared as part of our itinerary.'

'We bake our own.' The smaller gent, his nose less beaky than his brother echoed the other. The two nibbled like moles eating from their claws.

'Yes deario', the fat mother said, 'you eat up. Have a bicky.' Offering food was chance to get to know the girl. She saw she had no ring on her third finger, no ring to show that she was loved. She didn't belong to a man yet, looker though she might be. A person needed rings. She'd give her right eye to be as thin as that, but the girl needed brightening with a bit of jewelry. Her kiddies all had signet rings and bracelets padlocked with hearts. Cheap brilliants had a habit of leaving green marks on the skin, but were better than none. Eating pulled down barriers, she was the matey sort herself. She'd noticed Mallory's badge in his lapel. 'Work on the camp deario? On the staff like?'

59

'Yes Mallory, what is your job exactly? You didn't say', Hope said. She licked the icing from her fingers, one by one.

'I've booked you in' Mallory said, quickly lighting up again. 'A nice chalet. They let me off to fetch you.'

'But let you off from what? That's what I want to know.'

'What job dear? Kitchen work or outside? You got a tan, I reckon it's outside. My kids and I come every year to get our tan. The nosh is good as well.'

Mallory explained that as an executive he got time off. The gents folded their serviettes. They looked at Mallory with candour, warming towards the honest fellow. They said that seeing to the well-being of those enjoying a holiday was worthwhile employment. They explained their presence. 'We come here annually. We like it. They give us preference because we are old-timers.'

'They know us.' The quieter one gently took Hope's serviette. A personage like themselves she was accustomed to right ways. Pushing, smoking, gobbling were rude. True her clothing wasn't modest, but her voice, dislike of smoke and breeding compensated. A charming lady girl.

'Stop that bloody staring Herb.' Though stare he well might. The fat mother never got used to the sight of the gents. She watched out every year. Were they as tiny everywhere? And women, how about it? She saw them taking a shine to Hope. That girl was class for all her nakedness. The chap was not her Dad.

'But while you are working Mallory what shall I do?' Thoughts of Joanna kept returning to her. Joanna would be eating back in Putney. Cheese perhaps, followed by something sticky. Her chilly feeling of emptiness wasn't only hunger. It started at Victoria when expectations turned out differently. She still felt flimsy in spite of cakes and being stared at could be tiresome. When little Herb was sick it made a diversion. Everyone had a suggestion, a sip of fizzy lemon, some Smarties, put his head out of the window, fan him with Reveille. The gents said that excitement plus the stimulant of cherryade had bought a consequence. The lad was groggy. They offered tissues, having kept some to hold against their own beaked noses, speaking from behind the bunched pink squares, their brown eyes bright as their chocolate velvet suits.

'There's plenty on the go. Something to amuse one and all', said

Mallory. He wished that Hope would notice the loveliness of the country through which they travelled. 'See the hawthorn Hope. And horses, look.'

'Horses, where? I may not stay.' So far their journey was rotten. In Putney Mallory had been magnetic, called her moongirl, honey. At Victoria he wasn't anyone you'd look at twice. 'Is it much further?'

'I thought you liked the country. The green is a sight for sore eyes.'

She wished he would shut up. She made herself look out of the window because he'd arranged this trip, put on his suit. She'd left his string horse on her piano. The fields reminded her of Joanna again, and of the meadow with the stream and cow parsley, She loved the small white flowers that clustered umbrella-fashion over green spines, she loved the bitter smell. She used to gather armfuls of it, to decorate the mudholes where they hid their frog spawn, and threaded sprigs of it in their belts and hair. Large animals, the farmyard kind, were ugly, the cows, the pigs and sheep. She'd always longed to ride a horse, though the time with the hanky was her only experience. The hooves thundering over their heads could only have been cows. Joanna always was a coward. She'd been the same that morning, the same frightened look on her face. 'How can you leave without eating? You won't fit in, you'll see.' She shut her eyes.

The trippers started gathering their things. Soon they'd be cooling their feet in salty water, eating candy floss. The fat mother buttoned her kiddies into cardigans, wiping their cheeks with a spit-wetted handkerchief. She used her tail comb on their curls, before settling her own. Hope, deeply asleep like the little gents, missed the bustle of arrival. They were the only sleepers as the train drew in. They slept through shouts and screeching brakes. They slept through Mallory trying to rouse them.

Along the platform were young men dressed in red blazers, standing there to welcome them. Throughout the week the Campers would be in their care. Once you got off the train you ceased to be a tripper, you became a Camper and you had no more problems. These young men saw to everything. They lifted down each Camper from the train, making jolly cries to break the ice. To lift Hope down was a pleasure, her lightness, swirling skirts and lemon smell was a treat compared to the heavy ones. The gents scorned a helping hand.

'Who are those men Mallory?'

'Oh never mind them. They're only entertainers. They're supposed to keep the Campers cheerful, see to any problems. They see to the activities too.' It was a relief that the journey was over. The entertainers, youngsters under twenty-five, were useful in their way, they made a welcome. Jokes and back-slaps were appreciated by Campers, who tended to feel lonely on arrival.

The fat mother shook with glee. The mirth-makers were a cure, made her feel young and slim. The Dining Super had been there for years, he always had a special wink, a jest. Now he gave out balloons printed with Kiss Me and Yippee into the eager hands of the Campers. The gents refused balloons, jumping the steps of the waiting coach to sit by the driver, their heads just reaching above window-level. They liked to keep their distance. Though they were pleased when the Dining Super greeted them by name. The Dining Super was another worthy fellow and his job was paramount. For a week he'd see that home diets were forgotten, he'd make sure that the Campers' most deep-seated need was satisfied, he would keep them stuffed with food. From now on, decision-making and responsibility were left behind. The Dining Super and the entertainers would take over with the aid of the Camp programme. The gents observed that the sea had a rotten smell, noticeable from the station, it had a hint of drains and sour chips.

'What time is lunch then, Mallory?'

'The dinners start when we arrive. You've got a lovely chalet. The coach will take us right inside the Camp.'

'Excuse me deario. Is this your first time here? It's lovely. My kiddiewinks and me, we never miss.'

'I've never been.'

'Then sit along of us. You and your father too.'

'He's not my father. Friend, not father.'

'Friend then. Lovely. Sit along of us.' Friend and the rest of it. She wasn't born last week, she knew who was friends and who was something different. Another thing the mother knew was, sex was one big hoax. You got a lot of kids. She loved her kiddies, every dimple. Sex was over-rated. She'd sooner watch a film which didn't make you pregnant. The skinny girl could join them. Made a pleasant change. She smiled with friendliness and started humming. 'Hearts that are engines, painted green, Mouths full of chocolate-covered cream, Hands that can only lift a spoon, Everyone's gone to the moon.'

The gate attendant scowled as he lifted the barrier pole to let them in. His was the last frowning face on view. Inside the faces were all merry. Whatever the weather, whatever the time of day, smiles gay as masks were worn. The flags hung limply against the Camp flag poles and there were flying ants. There would be thunder later. The mother said that babies never cried in Camp, though there were a lot of all sizes. They ran about, shouting, eating, screaming but not crying. Various tunes were played from juke boxes and a crowd were queueing for bingo.

The heat, the strangeness, made her pale. She didn't like the flying ants that got in her hair. She peered into the mirror of a weighing machine. The little gents stopped by her elbow, noting her strange webbed fingers. How endearing. She told them that she had a sister, who wasn't quite a twin. They smiled enthusiastically. They pointed out the Reception Building where newcomers had to report. They said that paintwork was always blue or pink to match the hydrangeas growing round. The huge swimming pool edged with flags was coloured the same blue, the diving boards were pink.

'I'll have to leave you now', said Mallory. 'Must get back to work. Just follow. Book in, get your key. This is your receipt.'

'But Mallory, don't go. Please stay with me. I don't know anyone.'

'I can't stay darlingest.' He must leave the lovely girl and change out of his suit. It was a wrench, but he must be punctual. Once she had her key and her programme she'd fit in, be absorbed. He'd seen it happen, a shy outsider became a cog in the proceedings once they held their programme.

She hadn't decided what to call him and he was leaving her. The little gents had disappeared. She queued behind a traffic warden and a cleaner talking about the weather. The yellowing sky, the rumbles of distant thunder and the boredom of the jobs were topics to be hashed over. Hope had never discussed weather with anyone in her life.

'Stand here deario. I'm scared of thunder, would you bloody credit that? Stand in with my kiddies.'

'I am a bit scared too. I don't like flying ants.'

The fat mother said that her name was Lilian Pratt. She wanted Hope to have a chalet near her, for company like. The idea had

63

suddenly occurred to her; what the girl needed was a mother. 'Now no argy-bargy, I won't take No. Just leave it to Lil. I know the receptionist, I'll have a word.'

Lil leaned her arms across the desk. 'Just change the keys round dear. This young lady's come under my wing. She wants to be by me.'

The receptionist inclined her lacquered beehive-shaped coiffure towards the little group. She knew the regulars. A special smile for old timers was part of staff policy. She agreed with kindness if it didn't put you out, she gave them the keys, their programmes and the special metal badges worn by Campers. Her bee-stung lips were used to smiling, into the faces of campers or the telephone. A cheery word, a pat for kiddies, made for a pleasant holiday. She pointed out their way.

'I know, I know. Leave it all to me. Come Hopiewinks.' Now Hope was one of them. She didn't think she ought to chum up with the gents, she wanted her herself. She'd gained an older posh-talking child, a beauty, and thin with it. Who said miracles never happened?

The traffic warden and the cleaner went one way. Hope and Lil Pratt and the fat children herded past the swimming pool. Hope didn't mind; with Lil she wouldn't feel lost. It was like being fostered.

Lil explained the procedure. From now on you relaxed, you needn't think at all. You couldn't leave the Camp without a permit. No kiddy could get lost. It was a kiddy's paradise. 'And it's all hygienic. They don't allow no animals or blacks. We'll sit together in the Diner too. Cosy.'

'I have a sister back in London.'

'Sister eh? Lovely. Now where's your luggage deario?'

'I haven't any.'

'Not got luggage? You came down here without a stitch? You must give your Mum a headache. I'll lend you something.' She wasn't having one of hers bare-arsed.

The chalets were double-tiered, the upper stories reached by steps that rattled. Peoples feet rising and descending made a sound like 'para-dise – par-adise.'

'My sister is almost my age.'

'Fancy. Get on well, do you?'

'Yes. We're often taken for twins.'

64

'Twinnies? Where is she then, the other girl? I never fell for twins, thank Christ. I think the earth of my lot here.'

Doors along the corridor opened and shut like blue insect wings, revealing cleaners changing blue sheets for the new arrivals. On Saturdays everything got an extra wipe over. Mats were beaten, bins removed for scouring. Their bases had holes to prevent sticky bits adhering, and to prevent Campers using them for wrong purposes. There was a smell of Keatings. The relics of a week of fun got thrown away in time for the newcomers who rushed in to leave their mark, to make the chalets theirs and start the programme. Dreams were sweet in the blue chalets.

Hope looked forward to her own bedroom. The Camp was like Disneyland or a looking-glass world. Different tunes played without ceasing, crashes of machinery came from the rides in the fairground, children and adults screamed with joy, the steps kept rattling. They marked the lavatories Lassies and Lads.

Lil showed her where to wash. Each chalet had a bathroom, through a small blue door opposite the entry.

'A bathroom? Mine?' Her spirits rose. Her own bath would make the world of difference. Here she could escape from the noise and excitement into a blue room with frosted glass in the window and door. Here she could relax, pretend she was at home again.

6

The previous camper had left a cake of orange soap. On the glass shelf over the basin was a razor blade still in its film of paper. She had no towel. A towel was something a Camper was expected to provide. She soaped her cheeks with the orange soap, lubricating them. The light through the frosted window made her eyes almost look black. A soap-creamed skin made her feel calmer, more normal. She'd have to use the foot towel, a scrubby thing folded on the bath. She heard someone knocking.

'Let me in . . . darlingest.'

'Mallory? What do you want?'

'I came to see you were alright. You've moved your chalet number. What's that on your face?'

'Someone left some orange soap. I haven't got a towel.'

'I'll see to all that. I'll buy one. Leave it to E.M.' The helpless thing. She'd probably never made a bed in her life, or cooked a meal, she looked quite pale and shaky. He saw she was wearing Mrs. Pratt's cardigan. It looked bloody on her.

'What does "E" stand for?'

'Edwin.' He felt shy telling her. He was used to 'Mallory' by now. He said he didn't like it, forget that name, forget everything but that they were together again. He kissed her. He whispered 'You like me, don't you? You love me just a bit?' She was so lovely, so accessible. They could forget the annoyance of the journey, they were together. She looked at him docilely. He wiped the soap off, patting round her eyes with his hanky, kissing her soaped cheeks. He was so proud he felt that he ought to get paid. He'd got her there.

'Oh yes, I do. I'm sure I do', she said. It was a shame he smelled so smokey, like a boiler-room, but familiar. His tongue was familiar, the same old smokey taste, old friend, his hands were two more friends that loved and touched her. Outside the Pratts passed by, 'para-dise, par-adise'. Lil called out to hurry to the Diner. They couldn't wait to eat some more, to shove fresh food into their mouths. She wanted Mallory, her mouth was hungry. This was a paradise of food for the hungry.

'You're happy Hope? Say you haven't any regrets at coming?' He saw their profile in the mirror. She was blood-stock alright. He deserved payment. Her mother was a doctor, would she be prepared to cough? Might she pay for the return of her daughter? Pay him to release Hope from his thrall? Skill should be recognised, he'd write the Ma a letter. Not for nothing had his Uncles taught him to write a lovely hand. Hope's behaviour could be put to double advantage.

'Yes, yes', she said. Though something was missing, Joanna wasn't there outside, Joanna wasn't listening. She tried to put her mind to it. She felt the bumps under his flowing hair. He was trying to maze her mind, trying to kiss her step by step along the path. Soon she'd know the secret and be like Lady Chatterley and the ladies in the movies. He'd made another love-seat for her on the edge of the bath, a paradise of lips and teeth and smokey tongue and hands. What was Joanna doing now? Could you change the name of Edwin by deed poll? Was her nosebag alright? The towel was scrubby underneath her knees. The boiler-room was quieter.

He kissed her blissfully. This place was safe. No one could get out or in without a permit, the Camp was safer than a prison. 'Dear Dr. Greenham, your daughter and myself were made for each other. The possibility occurs that you might want her back. For a consideration this could be arranged. Signed from yours E.M.' Parting from her would be a real wrench. She was so nice.

The gong chiming over their heads alarmed her. A voice called a message about lunch. The sound came from a grid on the wall.

'What's that Mallory? How terrible.'

'It's the loudspeaker, that's all. It tells the Campers what to do. It backs up the programme, let's you know the time. Just the loudspeaker, not to worry', he said. He petted her to calmness, she startled easily. He had a weakness for nervous creatures. Foals, rabbits, weak-minded things brought out the kindness in his nature. The happiest times of his life had been with horses. He combed her with his own brown comb, making her hair shine. He asked her to give the cardigan back. The fat mother was not a person to borrow clothes from; he'd buy her all she needed. The Campers were a crude lot, mostly. He arranged to meet again at four. He advised her to stay clear of Mrs. Pratt, and kissed her long and suckingly till they met again.

The Pratts were a family for bows and brilliants in the hair. Their faces shone from washing and all had changed into frocks of flowery nylon pleating. Herb wore a pretty tie. Lil asked Hope where her cardigan was and explained that the Camp was divided into houses like royalty. Winning points for your house made you feel superior, like being back at school. The noise in the Diner was deafening but Lil loved it there. She had two tables placed together like a banquet. Food and her kiddies were her god. She'd always believed that a heavy child was happy and that stopping a whine with a bit of something tasty was better than a smack. Now Madam Lady Hope was one of hers she'd fatten her. While waiting for the soup they looked at the programme. It was drawn up by the Commandant who provided fun for every waking minute. Lil and her kids planned to play clock golf later. There were tennis courts and every kind of sport. Hope said she had to meet her friend, she didn't want to keep Mallory waiting.

'Mallory? Is that the name? Let him wait. He's bloody paying isn't he. You're under my wing now. Let him wait.'

The plastic trails of flowers hanging from the ceiling and the steam from the food obscured the vision. The tables were so congested that you had to shout. Waitresses and entertainers laughed good-humouredly though behind the serving hatch you could see a glimpse of cooks with furious looks on their faces. They clanged vats of beans and hissed chops onto hot plates. They weren't on show, their job was to ladle food out onto plates. A cook was highly paid, could afford to expose his real feelings. The Campers didn't care. The ceiling overhead heaved gently up and down beneath the feet of dancers in the Princess ballroom from whence music could be heard between the shouting and the clatter of dishes. Campers loved these conditions of eating, it made a change from the kitchen at home with only a radio. They called for more roast meat from the cooks and cheered when anything was dropped. Tables with lucky numbers won points for the house of Plantagenet. The Dining Super called 'Cuddle up now folks, trough time'. Lil lined each cup with a bedding of sugar before she poured the tea. Her kiddies spread ketchup on their bread, liking squidgy food. They rarely spoke except to mutter 'Wanker' or something crude.

'Of course the waitresses are Irish. Students and that, come over to make a bit quick. Your gent friend isn't Irish?'

'Of course not. At least, I hope not. I can't stand the way they carry on. Killing, bombing each other and all that religion. I can't eat that, I'm vegetarian.'

'Not eat pork? Faddy aren't you? Give the lady that one with the kidney Miss. A kidney is something that I relish.'

'I don't like meat. I'm not a farm-hand Mrs. Pratt. At home we eat sparingly. Cheese and a little fruit.'

'Call me Lil, and give your spuds to Herb.'

They talked about Mallory. Lil wanted to know how long they had known each other and what his job was. She hoped that he respected Hope. Some men were bleeders when it came to that. Her own man was stopping in London. Lil believed in lots of kids.

'And I do not. I never want any.'

'You can't be natural. A woman should ought to want kiddies. Her world is kids, whatever about wedlock.' Lil felt warm-willed towards Hope looking at her with eyes that didn't blink much. Fate had sent her the girl. She'd soon show her.

The little gents sat in the far corner among the elderly and handicapped. They liked to think they ruled this part, in their opinion this section was for the elite, where manners were observed, food eaten slowly, where water in a glass or extra jam were appreciated. They discussed Hope as they licked ice cream off their spoons. They didn't like to see her in wrong company, she ought to sit with them. They'd have a word with Super, with whom they were on chatty terms. The Super and one or two others had been there years ago when they'd done their tap-dance in the Princess ballroom. It was a peak day of their lives. The Campers had marvelled to see their small feet tapping so fast. Once was enough, they hadn't danced again. Life had taught them that miniatures, whether animals, people or ornaments, were valuable. They held their bodies in high regard. They watched the fat mother light a fag. Disgusting. Her children too were rude of mouth. Their new friend was palling up with riff-raff, her place should be with them. They made allowances for her mode of dress, she was, they judged, a lady in a quandary, a person unsure of her course.

'Smile duckies', the flashlight chappie ordered them, as he walked between the rows of tables. First meal pictures were popular. Only ten bob in a plastic case, it made a nice memento. The gents licked their withered lips into his camera.

Hope told Lil that she was going back to her chalet. She curled into a hump under her honeycomb quilt. The cotton smelled of glue. She slept with her wrists tucked inwards, oblivious to the campers' footsteps rattling up and down, or the voice from the loudspeaker. Loudspeakers were planted everywhere. Activities were announced throughout the afternoon. Birdie and Bert wanted beginners for an Olde Tyme practice in the Princess. Aunti Bow-wow would see the under fives for a puppy meeting. The Padre would like to meet Sunday communicants. Big prize bingo, bring your friends. Volunteers wanted for a life-saving class by the pool at three thirty. Hope's face got paler with sleep. Her left eye twitched. Her brain felt rested when she woke. She looked with pleasure round her blue painted room, with the curtained recess for shoes. Joanna would have liked the bathroom too. The bed was just right for two sisters. The night was a hurdle looming nearer. She wanted to be loved as much as she was afraid of it, she wished that she could stay in the chalet for a week with the door bolted. She got into the bath.

In the passage Campers were talking of the rainstorm that happened while she slept. They pegged their washing onto lines that stretched from posts supporting the overhanging roof and marvelled that rain could be so heavy. She had no clothes to hang out or take in, she'd solve the problem by washing frequently. If you washed a lot, especially the parts that smelled it was as good as changing clothes. The women pegging out their clothes had no fear of sex, their nights were not mysterious, they knew what to expect. She couldn't even remember Lavender's books in the Cloaks. She remembered Euphemia giggling 'Wunwun won a space race. Tutu won one too'. She would feel more confidence if she could step out in something exotic like a black halter-neck or shoes with diamond straps. The tin in her mothers desk had been old, used. Everyone changed clothes at night.

Dancing was most popular after the evening meal. The programme catered for all tastes. There was Olde Tyme, rock, limbo contests, country western and modern. Signposts pointed to the Lazy Lion, the Goat, the Beachcombers Bar where these activities were. An arrow pointed to the Padré's Quiet Place and Sing Along With Stan. Mallory was to meet her by the Camp Photographers. Machines in the amusement galleries clattered without stopping. Coloured fruits or film stars' faces lit when pennies were inserted. You rarely heard the winning crash of copper. Fortunes were told by electronic flickers that predicted nothing gloomy. Balls suspended on water jets, or ducks on string waited to be shot at with airguns. There were donkey rides. The Commandant's programme couldn't fail. Because he knew that eating was important as laughing there were kiosks selling snacks at every intersection.

Her skirts were cool against her scrubbed ankles. She skirted rows of chalets where families were changing. They buckled shoes, urinated, sprayed themselves with lotions, flanelled their young while Fathers read the programme. Then they emerged to stroll across the lawns to see what the flashlight chappie had been up to. His snapping was a riot. He'd snap you changing underneath a towel, he'd snap your naughty-naughty, he'd snap your dentures sticking in a bun, he had a sense of fun. He snapped the entertainers too, but not the Commandant. No one had ever seen the Commandant.

'Look Mum, the skinny cow. He snapped her and not us. Bleeding cheek.' Indignation made Lil's children talkative. They crowded round the pictures, pointing with fat forefingers at Hope's picture.

'What, our Hope? You're bloody right and all. She's eating nicely, she's eating like a queen.' The way Hope held her spoon showed her lot up something rotten.

'Here I am, Lil.'

'Enjoyed a good kip, did you deario? Come to see your picture?'

Hope went silent with pleasure. In the centre of the display case was her photograph enlarged. He'd taken her raising an icecream wafer to her mouth in a gesture of daintiness. Her eyes showed wide-spaced, her firm jawbone with the tips of her healthy teeth just showing had the look of a hunter reaching to eat. She was captivated by it, she couldn't look away. She made herself glance at the other snaps, the paltry people looking self-conscious over their plates, but her eyes couldn't keep away from herself, she was outstanding. That air of bewilderment was really sweet. In the bottom right corner were

71

the little gents smiling by their chrome teapot. They'd posed, were used to flashlight ballyhoo.

'I see you're famous', Mallory said, behind her. He'd noticed them already, was not surprised the chappie had singled her out. There was another smaller one, taken on arrival looking in the mirror of the weighing machine bewilderedly. He took her hand. He'd order half a dozen of the pics. His moongirl was acclaimed. 'Dear Dr. G. I enclose a picture of your girl. You know the price. I have more like them. Signed from yours E.M.' He asked her if she'd had a proper lunch and what she'd done in the afternoon. Hope said that she had slept and had a boiling bath.

'A bath? In the afternoon?' A bath once or twice a week was a healthy thing, or a daily swim. Hot water before going out in the air could be dangerous. Besides, he'd looked forward to giving her a rub-down himself, later on.

'We often do, at home.'

'We? Just who is "we"?' The only 'we' she ought to be thinking of was him and her. He could see their names on pillow-slips or personalised stationery. Some of that would come in handy.

'Joanna and I. We bath a lot at home.'

'You want to forget all that. You're here with me now. Your home is here right now, with me.'

'Joanna isn't "all that." She is my sister. We're close.' As close as Naomi and Ruth. Joanna's face should be by hers in the picture. Joanna should be holding her hand, not Mallory. The reason everything was beastly was because she wasn't there. Large splashes of wet fell onto her cheeks and throat, that felt like tears.

'Raining cats and kittens again. I gave her my own cardigan, but would she wear it? Not she. Fancy travelling here without a stitch. It's bloody mad.' Lil felt virtuous. A plastic mack was a necessity on holiday.

Hope's thin skirt felt like used carbon paper. Summer rain was wettest. She wished now she hadn't refused Joanna's offer of cash, as well as her burned toast. The sky had suddenly gone dark.

'We must get you under cover, darlingest. In out of the rain.' He didn't want her brooding over Joanna. Home-sickness would spoil his plans. She mustn't think about Putney and that sister, he'd have to split that little bond. If she started pining she wouldn't want to stay.

The Putney sister mustn't bollox things. He said that now was the time to show her where he worked, pulling her over the soaking grass. Their hands were slippery with rain. That Lil was a kindly sort, obviously, and meant well. But Hope needed excitement.

Inside the funfair enormous painted machines waited to give the Campers rides. Everyone liked danger as long as the entertainers were near to keep them safe. An illusion of peril was exciting. And rides were scheduled as part of the programme. They could ride at specified times on the new world satellite, the merry mixer and the big dipper. Mallory told her there was careful supervision, though the joysticks of the dodgems could cause minor accidents.

'Here we are then, this is my machine.'

'Is this the place you work. Good heavens. A roundabout. How simply lovely.'

'She's in my charge. You like her then?'

He walked Hope proudly round the roundabout in the centre of the funfair. It was the chief attraction, one of the biggest in the British Isles. He'd helped to renovate her; there wasn't a smoother ride in the country. This machine was the other love of Mallory's life. He almost felt shy of letting them meet. He enjoyed looking at Hope. He never tired of looking at his roundabout with the painted animals, their tails and manes picked out in gold. He'd always had a love of horses, including mechanical ones. He felt Hope would understand and share his enthusiasm. 'Let's walk round her again', he said.

'I'll have a ride. Which one is your favourite Mallory?'

'I never ride myself. I only operate. I couldn't stand the motion. You get up though,'

'I don't know which to choose.'

'I touched the manes up with paint before you come . . . came.' In spite of care wrong tenses slipped from his tongue. He had no time for people who spoke badly. His speech had helped him get the job with Miss Delicate. Speech was as important as cleanliness. He'd told the Camp he was a Baptist and not afraid of work. The testimony had proved a winner. Tending this machine was not work but pleasure. He told the lad who helped him run the roundabout to take a break, he'd take over the controls himself. He noted with disgust the bitten sandwich and oily rag on top of a comic by the switches. He never ate or read while on the job himself.

The animals were named on their tails. Bert, Perce, Vince, Reg, Ron and french names for the lady horses. Estelle, Francine, Juliette. They had red nostrils flaring above their opened mouths. Hope chose a black horse, Johannes. He had square teeth at the other end of forceful looking buttocks. Unlike the others his tail was chopped. There were some nameless cockerels for kiddies. Parents held their babies in front of them as they clung to the wooden poles twisting like barley sugar from the necks of the beasts up into the conical roof. Slowly they started rising and falling in time to the music. The riders began to hum. The tune they played was so catchy and suitable, about going to the moon, they couldn't help joining in. Round and round like a circular choir they travelled, gradually gathering speed. The opened mouths of the horses and cocks appeared to be singing too. The little gents who'd skipped up at the last moment hummed from their golden cockerel. The poles churned up and down, the outer, the middle and the inner circle moving at varying heights like a wave of golden manes and tails. Mouths gaped, eyes glared.

Hope clung onto Johannes' ears. Her yellow hair streamed out. It was like flying. She curled her toes round the black flanks under her. The roof shivered from the heaving of the poles.

'You'll get sick if you look up', Mallory called. He pulled a lever to reduce the speed. Her hair was heavenly, he didn't want her getting ill. It was a responsibility. You had to time the rides in case a child got sick.

'I'm staying here. I'll have another ride', she said.

The gents stayed on their cockerel. They noticed Hope on the other side of Mallory. It pleased them that they had so much in common with her. They planned to really get to know the lady girl, they would show her their ornaments and explain about their lives. They loved the roundabout, it was so innocent. That's what they liked about the Camp, its childishness and fun. They were dismayed by the current trend towards violence, the accent upon sex. These aspects of life offended them. The Commandant provided lamb-like activities for them to enjoy. They thought Hope looked delightful on the black horse, her carefree expression a contrast to the black fierce sensible one beneath her. She leaned forward, singing.

'Hope, please get down now', Mallory yelled. 'You've had enough.' A ride or two was fair enough, but she was taking things too far. She looked like someone making a votive act. People were staring. Her hair flew out so finely you could see the horses and the other faces through it. 'Please Hope, do you hear?' He was paying, he had some rights. He couldn't join her, he had to man the machine, and riding sickened him. Her shoulder blades stuck out, it wasn't nice not wearing underwear. That skirt was brazen. He'd buy her something decent right away. To watch her body made his stomach shiver. He had to light a cigarette, to settle him. He must stay calm and controlled. 'Dear Dr. G. Your daughter has been riding.'

When the gents got down, having enjoyed several rides, Hope followed them. She took no notice of Mallory but pushed after the gents, moving quickly through the crowd. Being small they were used to manoeuvering through a throng. They took no part in the programme's events, apart from riding. They liked to watch. The entertainers left them alone, they were privileged old timers. They greeted the senior campers by name as they passed their deck-chairs. It saddened the gents to see the seniors ageing each year, becoming careless with regard to crumbs and teacups, their speech deteriorating. They were thankful to be able to trot on their own four feet to their point of destination – the trampoline demonstration.

'Hope, don't go after those little chaps. Come with me. I'll take you to the rifle range.'

Children followed Hope and the little gents, lured from their kiddies corner. Seniors fancied watching it as well, fumbling over the damp grass to watch something difficult well performed. The gents knew that Hope was behind them. They saved a place by them in front of the trampoline. They squatted down contentedly. The young and the old Campers waited for the demonstrator to show them how to defy the laws of gravity. For once mouths stopped chewing.

'Now keep back all you lot. No hands on the frame. I don't want a single hand touching the trampoline frame. It's asking for accidents.' The young man took off his blazer. He smoothed his hair back. His large-jointed fingers had a supple curve. His ears were large and flat against his rather pointed skull. He had the relaxed movements of an athlete as he bent to pile his change on the ground by his blazer, his long limbs matching his height. His woollen socks had white soles. He vaulted up onto the canvas, starting with little jumps and gradually outdoing his momentum. He used his arms like wings to fly him

75

higher. The seniors and the kiddies gasped with wonder as he soared increasingly between each plunge. He started turning, a quarter summersault, a half and then a whole one. Next he did a double turn to land upon his chest before bouncing into a spiral. He bombed down with clasped knees. There was silence from the onlookers. The canvas creaked under the leaps of the man in the white tracksuit. The young were silent from admiration, the elderly were quiet with a wordlessness that came from sadness. They had no hope of such an achievement, their agile years were gone, they wouldn't be able to climb onto the frame, they could only watch with weakened sight. The gents' mouths jumped uncontrollably. They'd love to have a try. It was harmonious having Hope sitting with them.

7

Her ride on the roundabout had been a foretaste to the joy of watching the sportsman. A quill of black hair separated from his head to stick out blackly against the heavy rain clouds. She watched him slow down gradually, reverting to small jumping, slower, slow.

'What is his name?' she asked the gents.

'His name is John. He puts on demonstrations for kiddies. He is a master at all exercise. We heard Aunt Bow-wow speak of him as John.'

'His moniker is John. Aunt Bow said.'

'He's new to us. We never saw his kind: gymnastics worthy of the name. The athlete is a mystery. We only know his name.'

'New recruit.'

The gents took turns to tell Hope. They were as keen as she was. Watching John set their spirits free. They spoke in low voices, while their eyes moved up and down after the flying figure of John. They told Hope they'd seen her on the carousel, they also enjoyed a spin round, but on the whole they liked watching better than participating. A pair of life's onlookers, they liked to be *au fait*, would like to get to know her. Hope told them that she felt unhappy, she was sorry that she hadn't thanked them for their cake. The train journey had been horrid. She said she missed her sister. She said the Camp was not what she had expected from the brochures. They talked absorbedly, not noticing when John stopped. He put on his blazer and shoes and walked away, the children following. They copied his long steps. Their elders went back to their deck chairs. Hope and her new friends sat in front of a patch of clover leaves. Without thinking their hands groped in search of four-leaved ones. To find one would be an omen for a long friendship. Hope felt their sharp nails touching her. She asked them where they lived.

They spoke about their lives with pleasure. They disliked nosey parkers; Hope's enquiry was affectionate. They told her that they lived in a basement off Marylebone High Street. They kept to themselves, because they were tired of being the target of cocked snooks. This week at Camp was the only time they mingled with the world. At home they had each other; it was enough. They knew of others like themselves who joined circuses to become accepted, exploiting their size, allowing ladders and buckets of water to fall on them. They eked out their pension by making things. They had a connection with a shop in Marylebone that bought their dolls fashioned from matches, their furniture constructed from bus tickets; small airy objects suitable for dolls' houses. They collected things like eggshells, milk bottle tops, fish-bones for their odd-material toys. Apart from the one time in the Princess they had never put themselves on show. It was a great pleasure for them to touch Hope's hands, rooting in the clover for a four-leaf. It made them think that life still had something up its sleeve. They were proud of the toys that they made. 'That is our situation. Tell us, lovely dear, your own story. We have great concern for you.'

'We worry.'

'Worry? Why should you worry? I'm alright. I've got a sister, I told you. We're fond of each other, like you two.'

'Your travelling friend, the man with whom you came, is doubtless admirable, but he lacks vision. He isn't suitable. We may be small, but we observe. We have seen many things.'

'Loutish. We've seen a lot.'

'We feel that you should part. Do not pursue involvement. Take your leave of him.'

'Pack him in.'

'D'you think I ought to? I'm not exactly keen on him. I'm sure it isn't love.' Since seeing John the Sports her feelings for Mallory had dwindled into non-existence. Tall John the Sports tumbling through the damp air had been divine, he'd tumbled from the sky into her life. She told them about Joanna back in Putney, who she missed, and about the rabbit and their mother who wore hornrims and had asthma. The gents hung on her words, nodding their heads. It was all so interesting. Putney was a lovely spot in summer, they believed. Their fingers went on twisting through the thin green stems. She didn't love the lout. What a good job.

'I only came for a short break, to see if I like it', she said. Talking to

78

the gents was relaxing, made her forget about the coming night and sexual nervousness. Their listening ears that nodded up and down had a calming effect. Like confessing to a priest, it made her feel better. She asked if they were fortune tellers or had to do with magic. They told her that they didn't do official readings, they told the tealeaves, each other's mostly. Vibrations should not be ignored. They looked across the green as Mallory came over. Their mouths straightened with distaste.

'There he is again. Your travelling companion is beckoning. He looks impatient.'

'His dander is up.'

'Hope, what on earth are you playing at . . . darlingest? It's supper time.' How humiliating it was to be ignored. The Campers would think Hope preferred the roundabout, the sporting demonstration or chatting with the freaks to being in his company. What was she doing, jabbering on the grass?

'I sit with Mrs. Pratt and her family. She keeps a place at her table.'

'I know. I've fixed things so that I can sit there too. For tonight at any rate.'

'Hey you two! Aren't you ever bloody coming? The rest have started eating. It's roast turkey. They give us roast turkey of a Saturday. We'll miss the nicest bits, the breast and that.' Lil was charmed to welcome Mallory to their party. A man was always acceptable. She'd make sure to sit opposite. Exciting. She hadn't felt so keyed up since she'd glimpsed King Farouk before he passed away. She was getting of the opinion that Hopiewinks wasn't as wishy-washy as she seemed. It could be she was fly. The way she'd stared at the sportsman chap, eating him with her eyes. The way she'd parleyed with the midges in the grass, holding hands. Was her Hope on the make? She'd ask her straight, 'I say old deario, have you two had it up yet?' She'd pick her moment, people told her things, it came with being fat.

'I'm Mrs. Pratt', she said to Mallory. 'We met before, remember?'

'I'm Edwin. First names here.' He settled his feet under the table. He passed the bread and butter to the kids. This was better. Hope liked the Pratts. 'Alright darlingest?'

'Well, I'm Lilian.' Lil enjoyed pronouncing the syllables, a classy name gave you importance.

79

'You're Lil to me. You dancing later?' Mallory ignored the children eating. They lacked savvy. Common and fat they might be, but an improvement on the freaks. A civil word was never wasted. He'd be cordial. The kiddies couldn't help their girth, inherited no doubt.

'We frequent the dancehall of an evening. Do you dance deario?' Lil looked at Hope. The girl appeared half-looped, pushing vegetables about in her ministrone and staring. She'd been staring from the start, at pigeons on the platform. A bad sign, staring. She asked her if there was anything wrong with the soup.

'I'm a vegetarian. I quite like dancing. Free expression. The Martha Graham style.'

'Martha who? I fancy the tango myself. My Jim was once a medaller. Do eat that soup, Hope.'

'You mean you don't enjoy the rations darlingest?' Costing him good cash and choosey with it. What a liberty.

'She'll feel peckish in her own good time. Meanwhile we won't waste it. What is this free expression Hopie?'

'It's doing what you like to music.' It was leaping round the school with Lavender, knowing that Joanna was near. It was twisting your body into ridiculous shapes of letters while you dreamed of love. You bent, you swayed, you stamped or made a face. Joanna I miss you.

'Sounds lovely deario. But in the Princess they do the tango. D'you fancy tangoing Ed? You coming? How's about it Hopie?'

'Alright.' She wanted Joanna to dance near her. She wanted to ask if John the Sports would be there.

'Hope's mother is a doctor', said Mallory in a loud proud voice.

'Lovely. Yes, she told me.'

'Got a sister too. Like as two peas aren't you Hope?'

'Yes, we are alike.' Joanna you sweaty-handed sister warming butter up with sugar, where are you? Scribbling poetry, messages on rubbers, I want you. I hate the noise, I hate the soup, I hate the people, I need you.

'A sister is a lovely thing. 'Course as I said the Camp is for families. There's nothing here to harm a kiddie's mind. You'll like it in the Princess.'

'Wait until you try my partnering. I'll take a turn with you both.' It wasn't his habit to be churlish. The fattest slattern had a use; a place in life. Lil wasn't half a bad sort, was helping Hope to get used to the place and forget the sister back in Putney. She made him feel less nervous.

Lil said she'd take him up on that. They'd show the Camp what real tangoing was. She told them about the midges tapping years ago. She'd heard about it from the Super, though not seen it. Those small feet clicking to a melody would have equalled King Farouk. Life was full of lovely things, didn't Ed agree? Mallory said he'd show her how to creep. He spooned his pudding up with relish and lit a cigarette.

Hope stared in outrage as she started coughing. She felt the tears coming. Had Jo been there she would have thumped her on the back.

'You're coughing 'cos you don't smoke. Allergic to the fumes most likely', said Lil, lighting up a king-size. 'Your lungs are hyper-sensitive.'

'Take it easy, darlingest. You'll make yourself ill', said Mallory. He squeezed her knee-cap. She was making an unnecessary fuss and calling attention to herself again.

She couldn't stop it. Through wet eyes she saw the little gents. They nodded over from their corner, sending sympathy. How filthy to smoke at table. Were she sitting with them nothing so vulgar would happen. Both imagined that they patted her with loving hands.

'Do stop it darlingest. The champagne draw is next. Try to stop, it's only in the mind.'

The champagne draw was every week, to round off the turkey and sprouts. Lil said it was the real thing, none of your bloody perry, it was a weekly ceremony, the table with the lucky number got the hooch. Five hundred heads turned to watch the Super spin the arrow on the wall. He laughed and shouted that the stuff in his bottle was guaranteed to turn some lucky Mummy and Daddy Camper on. Which lucky Mum would be settling her nightie next morning while Dad collected the morning cuppa? 'And the lucky table is . . . table . . . one one three.'

'Ooooh goody goody. Hope and Ed you must have brung us luck.' Lil's heart felt melted with the pleasure of it. Her adopted daughter was lucky. There was plenty for them all.

The cork flew. The Campers clapped as Super poured the drink.

'Give us. Give', screamed the children stretching out their cups.

'Congratulations table one one three, may your week be double sunshine, double spree', said Super formally.

81

The children squeaked and wiped their lips. Lil said she relished bubbly. Some bubbly would soon put paid to Hopie's cough.

'A seal on our togetherness', whispered Mallory before drinking.

'Give us. Give.'

'Very civil of you. Don't mind if I do', said Super gratefully.

'An excellent vintage', said Mallory. He was partial to good wine, he had the know-how. He asked if Hope liked it. He was pleased that she'd stopped coughing.

'It is quite nice. Yes.' Hope sipped it quickly. Her eyes dried Her throat eased. She sipped again. 'It is nice. Very.' Champagne was a drink of promise and rejoicing. She took a few gulps and her anxiety went. The meal was like a wedding celebration. Such a happy crowd, with Lil so friendly and the children quaffing. The Super said that winning counted as a house point for Plantagenet. Lil said she looked a different girl, she had a bit of life in her face.

'A good year this. Only the best for you Hope', said Mallory.

'Hope is a peculiar name deario, if you don't mind my saying. I give my lot flower names, barring Herb, though Herb's a flower too.'

'They called me Ernest once', said Mallory.

'Ernest? Ernest Mallory? When was that? I love this stuff. Can I have more?'

'Just say the word. It was back in the West Country as a lad. Stable lad. A classy place, titled. I learned a lot. A handy experience.'

'Ernest is a beautiful name. I fancy it', said Lil.

'Tell me more about your family Mallory.' The drink gave Hope a floating feel, she fitted in at last. They accepted her. Kind Mallory, filling and refilling her glass with Camp champagne and fondling her knee.

'No family. No immediate family. My uncles brung me up, I told you. I've had to make it on my own.'

'Banana boy deario? Shame. A kiddy has no choice, yet they say there's a god of love. My lot have taken a shine to you don't worry. Names of flowers, every one.' Lil burped, remembering to pat her mouth. She'd learn her lot to say pardon and ta if she had to choke them.

'Not Barnardo. Reared by uncles. Travellers, I told you Hope, remember?'

'But you were orphaned.' Hope looked at him. She felt motherly.

Poor chap, deserted. She took his hand. 'You have me now. You have Lil Pratt and her kids. You're needed and respected. You keep the roundabout going. They rely on you.'

The Pratt children giggled. Lil snapped at them to shut their cake holes, had they no feeling? Some people would giggle at a funeral. She was soft-natured herself. A slow tear rolled down her fleshy cheek because he was an orphan. For two pins she'd take him in her own home. They'd all meet in the Princess to round off a lovely night. The turkey had been perfect. Mallory shook the bottle over her cup.

The gents liked the Princess, the ballroom over the dining hall. Up here the same corner was reserved for seniors. There were tip-up seats and dimmed lights for those who only watched. There were always more watchers than dancers in the Princess and Birdie and Bert didn't pester you to take to the floor. They were understanding, they knew the gents could shimmy if they wanted, their years didn't preclude them, it was simply that their energy was better directed elsewhere. There was ample space beneath the seats for crutches, cardigans and the various remedies used by elderly people. The gents' hair looked a picture against the chocolate-coloured tip-up backs. They liked to go there every night to look.

'You're sure you meant the Princess, Lil? Bit fuddy-duddy isn't it?' Though Mallory didn't really object. He could dance with Hope without fear of her being snatched. He could put his arm round her lovely waist, a public furtherance to their relationship, blessed by old eyes and smiles.

'A waltz now, Campers, shall we?' called Birdie.

'On the floor now. Everybody on the floor, except the kiddies.' Kiddies weren't encouraged by Bert. He hated them. Where there were Mums, kids came. Lil's lot of kiddies were quite loathsome. The sight of them on his polished floor made him feel murderous. They wouldn't be caught. They made the Campers nervous, not liking to risk it with them sliding. They ruined his polishing. He felt his age when the youngest kicked him on the shin.

The seniors waited. Tapping a foot to the music was as good as dancing. Watching was restful, especially when you forgot the steps. They saw Bert getting kicked. They knew about swelling and veins. Bruised shins could be nasty.

'Dance darlingest?' Mallory put out his arms. Their wedding dance. His partnering would make it ritual fire. His heart bumped.

'Come beauty, give yourself. Let's waltz.'

He led her to the floor. The Danube waltz was easy, she'd picked it up. A one-two-three in short revolving steps. 'That's it Hope. Relax. Just give yourself to the music.'

'But it's archaic. I prefer to dance by myself, Mallory, thank you all the same. Shall we stop?'

'Alone? But you've got me. This is the Blue Danube.'

'That's just it. Can't they play something less stilted?'

'Stilted? What can you mean Hope? Relax.' If anyone was stilted it was her. He'd seen her in Putney waving her limbs, supple, willowy. Now she was stiff as a board. It would take a superman to push her. Appearances were misleading; she couldn't dance a step. 'Liking it any better yet?' He tried to keep from pleading. She was so wooden.

'Not very, no.' Her champagny feeling was disappearing. If only he were John. If only John could show her and not Mallory smelling of smoke, crunching his feet on top of hers. The way he pumped her hand towards the centre of the floor like a piston was not at all romantic. They were the only two dancing.

'That's it, that's the way my bird', he said, dodging the Pratts. 'Dear Dr. G. Your girl has talent, a dancer in the making. Under my tuition she will excel. My predicament is cash. You understand that only lack of the ready causes me to pen this note. Signed from yours E.M.'

'Oh can't we stop it Mallory?' She didn't want the gents to go on looking at her, their eyes sending boosting messages of encouragement. They wished they could liven up her feet. They could feel the touch of her pale sweet hands among the clover. A lady girl as sensitive as that needed privacy and patience. They'd love to show her. What highjinks they could have with her to make a threesome. They rubbed their hands sadly. They willed her to loosen at the knees and count.

'Er . . . darlingest. You brought some nightclothes did you?' It bothered him. No prude; he had a sense of fitness. A young lady's titties, parts of intimacy, should be covered before unveiling. A button here, a rustle in the dark, were part of the occasion. Stripping the shell off the nut would give him courage to do what had to be done to the kernel. He felt like a green lad. 'Sorry mates', he muttered to an

84

old couple who had decided to brave it on the floor, in spite of kids. They kept their macks on as they circled gravely.

'What?' Hope kept her eyes on the door behind the gents. John the Sports stood there, miraculously.

'Clothes? I said have you any night clothes?'

'What are you on about? I've none. I told you.' She hadn't a toothbrush. She wanted John to notice her, but not while on the floor. She wanted to get away from Mallory badgering her about nighties. If Joanna had been there she wouldn't be in this position.

'We'll go to the shop. I'll buy you plenty.' Investing in her added to her value. She was so delicate he ached inside.

'I'll stay here with Lil. You go. It's wet again outside.'

'Alright'. He checked his wallet. This was coming pricey. He'd trick her in satins like a trousseau. That Dr. G. had neglected her duty.

'Where's Ed bloody going to?' Lil felt let down. Ed wasn't the fancy stepper he'd made out and Hope was a beginner.

Rain blew through the windows wetting the faces of the seniors as they sat watching. Unable to dance they hadn't the agility to move away without help. They didn't complain, a splash of rain didn't mar the general paradise.

John called the Pratt children to help him close the windows. They admired him. The Pratts needed leadership, someone chivalrous to copy. John spoke to every senior, asking names, listening to their symptoms. He liked making them comfortable. He questioned the advisability of so much noise and exercise for older folk. The food, the jokes and slogans were too rowdy. The programme didn't allow for intellectual interest, he'd like to suggest chess or quiz games for the seniors.

'That's John over there', Hope said. She waved. Needles of rain ran down the panes. His hair shone wetly, drops clung to the wool of her sweater.

'You know him then? You fancy him? I saw you watching with the midges when he was jumping. My kiddies love him too.'

In the shop Mallory moved from counter to counter. He felt shy.

'Shopping for your better half?' the assistant asked.

'No, girlfriend. Have you anything stripey?' Striped finery for her fine body, delicate wrappings to unwrap. She offered him a warm black jersey. He didn't like to ask for garters, or those bras with see-through centres. The slogan-printed panties offended him.

'I'll have a bottle of that.' He pointed to a display of perfumes. 'Wild Grass' sounded nice. Enamel rings were arranged on velvet, patterned in a leafed design. He imagined pushing one against the skin of her third finger while choir boys uttered hymns. Carried away by the beauty of a wedded future he chose a blue-dialled watch. 'For the cocktail hour' the label said. She liked receiving gifts. He'd not forgotten her delight in his string horse, was making another in black for her, with her name. If she liked horses she should have them. He chose slippers for her prancing feet, though prancing scarcely described their performance on the dance floor. The slippers were cosy. He'd teach her to tango, enter comps. Their marriage would be one in the eye for Dr. G. who should be shot for letting her run naked. As an afterthought he bought a poncho, large and thick as a horse's blanket. He wouldn't have his moongirl shiver. He asked the assistant to parcel them well as they were presents. He couldn't wait to watch her open them. He'd spent a lot.

His arms were full as he walked back through the rain. It thundered on and off, but not enough to be alarming. He'd carry her off to their love nest very soon.

With eyes still dazzled from the lights over the perfume counter he thought he was seeing double. There were twin girls standing on either side of Lil, two long-haired scrawny beauties shouting with identical mouths across Lil's astonished face, two voices bickering louder than the band.

'I might have guessed you'd follow me and spoil things. Piss off.'

'But you brought nothing. You must have clothes Hope. You came unclothed.'

'I knew what I was doing. Poking in. You're not wanted you prat-faced les.'

'You need your clothes, I'm not sorry I came, so there.'

'I am. Piss off and take that alarm clock with you. Clocks. One thing I don't need is time. It's time all day here through loudspeakers.'

'Well pardon me I'm sure, don't bloody mind my face. You come in waving an alarm clock without a with your leave. I take it you're Hope's sister. There's such a thing as manners.'

'Lil this is my sister Jo. Come to interfere as usual.'

86

'I'm Lilian. Lil to my friends. Pleased, I'm sure. What name did you say dear?'

'Joanna. I've brought my sister her luggage. She's used to having me look after things.'

'Very nice too. A blow by the sea makes a change. You must meet my kiddies. Staying very long are you?'

'Now that I've come I'm staying.'

'No, you're not. Piss off and take the next train back.'

'Hoity-toity pardon the French. Why don't we talk things over? Have a cuppa in the Lazy Lion. There's Edwin there, all flummoxed. You've given him a turn. What you got there Edwin? Presents?'

'Er . . . dearlingest. Er . . . look.' He cursed the rain that made his presents drip. He cursed Joanna. He cursed Hope for taking no notice of his gifts. 'Look dearlingest, I bought you this nice watch. An engagement present.' He set the parcels down in a tip-up and unwrapped the watch from it's velvet box.

'Engagement? Engagement for what? Hope, why is Mallory buying you watches? Let's get out of here. Come on.'

'Ooooh. A beautiful time-piece. Edwin Mallory you never bought that watch for Hopie? A time-piece fit for royalty. Just look.'

'D'you like it dearlingest? Say you do. Say yes.' He'd planned to offer it in bed, to put it round her wrist after the union rite, a thanks-offering. Instead, he held it after her retreating back.

'Ed, would you bloody credit that? Ignoring your gift. How downright rude, your lovely time-piece. And they supposed to be gentry.'

Lil and Mallory saw the sisters leaving the Princess, they didn't say goodbye or nod to the gents, they went on quarrelling their wide mouths twisting in acrimony. They kept invective as a kind of patois for times of stress, for tricky situations or when making a bolt. It disguised relief and pleasure, a cover for a spiritual embrace. They went on snarling, as their ankles splashed through the rain-soaked grass. Far-off thunder rumbled. At the bottom of the rattling steps they went quiet. Alone, they could settle.

'Mallory looked like a rat offering river weed.'

'Yes, he did. Our bathroom is rather nice. You'll like it. Did you bring peppermints?'

'Yes. What's the food like?'

'Awful. I'm still vegetarian. The place is full of rude postcards and children. They took a photo of me. There's a man called John.'

They shut the blue door. Thunder came closer, blocking the announcement on the loudspeaker requesting that Edwin Mallory should go to the reception block.

'I missed you. What made you come so soon?'

'The thunder. I guessed, this afternoon.'

8

'Pay no mind. Don't let on you care Ed. That's my advice.' Lil made him sit by her. Poor man, engagement watch still in his hand.

He said it was the disappointment of it that he minded; she hadn't even looked at the watch. A slap in the face. Lil said again he should ignore her. Were Hope truly one of hers she'd wash her mouth out. Money and brains were as may be, but there was such a thing as gratitude. He couldn't take it in. Unfair. By now her ravishment should be under way, instead of which he sat with Lil, while rainwater dripped from his turnups. Lil told him there were plenty bloody more, he shouldn't go after her, though dearie knew he'd good cause. Those presents and a pricey holiday. He'd not received so much as ta, much less his pound of flesh. Things would look brighter by morning, meanwhile he was welcome to confide in her, to let off steam. She'd be happy. That's what a woman was on earth for, to make a man feel wanted. True, she lived for her kiddies, but a man made that bit extra. Them chalets could be lonely on your own. Yet they talked of a god of love.

'I think I hear them calling me. I'm wanted in reception', he said.

The gents in their pink chalet on the far side discussed the unexpected arrival of Hope's sister. They couldn't have wished for anything better. Hope had doubled, now they were four.

'I believe the younger one has come to rescue our friend. They do not seem at ease. Both on the threshold of life's highway, yet I feel them bordering on a *mauvais quart d'heure.*'

'Bit of bother in the offing.'

'And how alike they are. Such beauty is delectable.'

'Oh quite.'

The two made ready for bed, helping each other considerately with difficult buttons, plumping their pink pillows.

In the blue chalet Joanna pulled clothes from a golf bag. Hurling the familiar Putney things to the floor kept her occupied when she asked the vital question. The floor was strewn with coloured tights and scarves. 'How far does it go in, Hope?'

'Oh nothing's happened yet, you may be pleased to know.'

Joanna felt consoled that Hope was the same, still her sister in ignorance with regard to carnality. She might be better looking, clever, popular or confident, had probably seen and felt the weapon of Mallory. She hadn't had it in her. She guessed it would be the colour of uncooked rabbit.

'*She* created hell about the rabbit after you went. Its fur is dangerous for her. She'll look after it while we're here though. Decent of her. I felt a bit sorry.'

'Sorry for her?'

'It can't be much fun. Fur makes her ill. She's lonely, though she is so busy. Tell me more about this place.'

'I've made these friends, two dwarves actually. They are so nice. And Lil whom you've met. John demonstrates the trampoline. He's in charge of sports.'

'Trampoline?' Joanna saw that Hope's expression became dreamy at the word, the way she'd looked before her trips to the boiler room, the look she didn't trust.

'It's heavenly. You jump on it. It's canvas stretched out on a frame. John's like an acrobat.'

'It doesn't sound much at all. I hate all violent sport. It's showing off. What else?'

Hope showed her the programme. Neither approved of so much noise and jolliness. She told about the champers and her cough at table. She was pleased to see her white string horse emerging from the golf bag. Together they admired it, standing it by them in the light of the bedside lamp. Their mother had told Joanna that they must make up their own minds about their careers and future. She had entire confidence. She sent no love or message. They got into the blue bath, making it like home, with peppermints and steam. They might get jobs in Marks and Spencer, go to pottery classes or make Christmas cards. They put the alarm clock under the bath. They forgot the other Campers, Lil next door with her family, the gents and Mallory. Rubbing orange soap into themselves, making plans, they were secure. If the present was happy you postponed worrying about the future. The hot water made them heavy. They got into bed.

Joanna curled against the back of sleeping Hope. Hope never dreamed or threshed in her sleep. She dreamed that Hope rode in a circle of white string horses, round and round, before breaking away, sailing up towards the skies. Her horse went black, the ones below melted into a swimming pool where children stared at Hope, and dwarves with naked bodies splashed the water, shouting at her. The collarless dog from Putney barked 'All those with infirmities can piss off. The pool is reserved for muscle development. Obey the queen.' Hope laughed down, spitting a deluge of spit. 'I am unbeatable. Obey your queen.'

Without opening her eyes she knew that someone was outside the door, shuffling at the handle, turning it. She'd meant to lock it. She kept her arm round Hope, quite still. Someone was opening the door. A silhouette was standing against the black, an outline like a bottle, slightly rocking. It was an armless bottle-shaped man coming in slowly. He held a bottle in his hands before him, moving quietly, rocking. He closed the door.

'Get out. Get out at once. D'you hear me? Go.' Hope mustn't wake and see him. She'd be afraid. 'Do you hear? Get out.'

'It's vodka. I've brought you some vodka. You'll like it, try it. You must drink.' But why were there two girls in the bed? The vodka in him was making him see double. His darlingest had doubled while his back was turned. How could he service two? What was this? He detested self-indulgence, but one over the eight was excusable under these circumstances. A drop for Hope would put things right. She had enjoyed her taste of bubbly, now for a taste of vodka. He'd give her the watch, get down to official business. His tool was right for it. There was an interloper in the bed. Another swig. Silence was golden, he mustn't splash or let it gurgle. Manners. This second girl was a puzzler. 'Who are you second girl?'

'What's happened? What's the matter? What's going on? Joanna, Jo. Joanna stop him. Joanna help me.'

'Drink this, I tell you. Drink it down. You must.' Force them to drink, compel them. He was the boss, the boss-man, rider. Show her, show the girls. Who were they? Undo buttons, show them, push the bottle in. Open you girl, you other girl, open, take what I have. I have

91

supplies of drink. Drink my bottle, drink it, put it in. Open, open your mouths, your legs, take it. Drink you girl. Other girl. Obey. I'm in charge. I've paid. I'll plug you, prick you, fix you. I want. This isn't what I want, this isn't what I had in mind. Darlingest . . . I didn't mean. "Dear Dr. G. I hope . . . I'm s . . ."

*   *   *

'Good morning Campers. Rising time. Up out of bed. Another happy day and fun ahead.'

The sheets were torn and patches of blood and drink had dried on them. The girls lay crossways over the bed. Joanna hadn't saved Hope. The string horse had fallen by the bottle and a patch of sick on the floor. Its legs no longer pranced, its tail was limp as a red wisp. There was an acrid smell coming from the stickiness on their limbs. Hope's eyes looked mad, staring with fixed blue glare at the wet patches. She didn't move. Joanna made her get up, pushed her onto a folding wooden chair while she pulled the bedclothes off. She stuffed them under the bed. She moved with jerks. They sat on the bare mattress. She remembered the dettol in her golf bag. The most important thing was secrecy. No one must know of this, no one must find out. The label on the bottle said use for abrasions. There was nothing about criminal assault. Bathe with warm water, a capful to a tumbler. Apply neat for insect bites.

'Get in the bath, Hope. Soak yourself.' A patient in a state of shock must drink weak tea.

'You get in with me Jo.'

'I'm going out for tea. Tea will restore us. Stop whimpering.'

'Jo don't go.'

'Shut up and get in the bath. Put in plenty from the bottle.' The smell was pleasant, a spiced country smell.

In the queue for tea were all the Pratts in dressing gowns, their faces greased from the heaviness of their sleeping. Lil was the sort to sleep through an atom bomb. She blamed her heavy sleeping on her pregnancies, the act taking place without her knowing. 'Where is Hope, deario? Are you two alright?' The younger girl was pale. Had the two had a punch-up in the night? Or had they heard the shocking

92

news already? 'You've heard then Jo? You've heard about it have you? Does Hopie know?'

'What?'

'The news about poor Ed.'

'What news please? What are you talking about?'

'It's shocking. You can only bloody call it shocking. He wasn't all that old.'

'What's shocking? Tell me please.'

'I never thought he'd turn to that. He must have done it from a broken heart.'

'Done what?'

'Your sister. He did it on account of her. He strung himself up in the one of the Lads. He was found early. Cut him down too late. Shocking. You don't expect that class of thing, a Sunday too.'

'Where was it?'

'The far side of the Camp. The pink chalets.'

'He's really dead?'

'Dead alright. Stiff as a brick. They had to cut him down.'

Joanna ran from the fat row of Pratts. Hope wanted her. She rattled up the paradise steps. Hope needed her, she'd have to break the news. Ed dead. Ed is dead, he wet the bed. He's dead. And when she saw her sitting on the mattress her face showed that she'd heard. She'd heard the Campers talking.

'Hope stop that twitching. Stop twitching your face. It's happened.'

She heard Lil coming up behind her, eager to be in on it. 'Nice thing of a Sunday. Both of you so quiet, not a sound all night. What a thing to wake up to. Where ever are your blankets? Hope will get cold. She looks sick to her belly already.'

'She's had a shock, you see. I must look after her, Mrs. Pratt.'

'Poor man and his watch. I expect Hope is sorry now.' Eating supper, dancing, out buying watches for the girl. He'd bought the mare a lot of clobber, Lil felt sorry for him, though usually she took the woman's part. It looked as though Hope wouldn't require her now. She had her young sister. What a let-down, her nice new daughter gone. And that poor Ed. She couldn't get the thought of him out of her mind. With his tie, his eyes all popping. Nasty. It was back to her kiddies on her ownio.

'Hope, stop that shaking. He's gone and that's the end. We'll

93

have to get away.' No one must find out. Hope smelled, a smell of dettol and the awful bed smell. Hope smelled like a station cloak room. She shook her to make her move and speak.

'He killed himself', she croaked at last.

'I know. But look what he did before that. He attacked us.' Once Hope began to accept it they could plan. Mallory was better six feet under than raping and slaughtering. Mallory was a barbarian.

'I never should have come. I wish I hadn't.'

'Well it's too late now, you did. The man was mad I don't know what you saw in him. He's gone.'

'What shall we do?'

'I don't know yet. Our mother must stay out of it. I'll write.'

They were equally involved. Hope knew no more than her about the secret act. A nightmare haze of pain, struggle and fright. News of suicide on waking.

'I want to go back to Putney, Jo.'

'We can't. That's what we can't do. Stop complaining and stop that twitching. Have you gone spastic? Your eye keeps twitching. Stop.'

'What do you mean?'

'Your left eye keeps twitching like a spastic.'

Hope's shocked face changed to one of incredulity. She looked over to the mirror. Elopement, rape and suicide within twenty-four hours and now a palsied eye, moving without her volition. It was unendurable, it made her look malign, a witch. She covered up her face, leaving the eye showing, it's corners pinned between her hands. The happenings of the night had turned her into a freak.

'Will it stay, Jo?'

'Shut up. It will recover. But what should we do next?'

'You're sure of it?' Her experimenting, searching for experience had only brought blackouts, blood and boss-eyes.

'We'll leave this room, we'll go.'

'Where to?'

'I've paid for my own chalet on the far side of the Camp. We'll take our things there. Leave your eye alone.'

It was quicker to throw things into a dressing gown than re-pack the golf-bag. Fluffy sweaters, Hope's long skirts, books, the recorder rained through the air. The alarm clock stayed behind with the string horse and the clothes Hope had worn the day before. They'd start off fresh from the chalet on the far corner. Put dead Ed out of their minds. Joanna said they should thank Lil as they passed her door. They smiled with bruised lips at her and her fat children. Lil called out that if they needed a pal they mustn't forget her. Joanna made her legs move confidently down the rattling steps, because Hope looked to her for leadership. She wondered if they ought to see a private solicitor or the Padre of the Camp whose name was Shake. Above all the matter mustn't get about. She would write back to Putney saying all was well. Notes and letters had been the start of all the trouble.

Campers were looking forward to Sunday breakfast. A smell of coffee hung about. Catholics likened this to incense, smiling with radiance. Soon they would be giving praise with Padre Shake who welcomed all sects. The girls bumped their bundled clothes through the knots of Campers assembling for the walk over the grass to the Diners.

The gents had bought a Times to look at while they ate kidneys and marmalade. They knew about the tragic loss. They mourned Mr. Mallory. The chap was now in Abraham's bosom. Beneath their looks of glum commiseration they were glad. One less bother in the world. Their Hope had made a lucky escape. They rarely envied the fully grown, neither their marriages, their kiddies nor their affairs. They saw the families having a lark on holiday, but in Marylebone they saw a different side. Wives hitting other ladies, mothers raising the voice to kiddies in a rage, dogs' messes in halls, husbands' nasty socks, social workers knocking. They saw the sisters with their bundle going to the pink chalets, the section kept for seniors, the ill or last minute bookings. The four of them together was a good job.

The pink paint here was shabby. Weeds grew in the crazy paving and windows of the single-storied chalets wouldn't open. There was no individual plumbing. Dead wasps lay along ledges and the rooms were not too clean.

'This is much better', Hope said, lying on the dirty counterpane. A sour smell came from the bin, containing old aspirins, peach stones and a glove.

'You can't flop yet. We're not in the clear, you know. When is your period due?' Once their cycles had coincided, before Mallory had entered Hope's life.

95

'I don't know. Some time in the week I think. Why? Jo, you don't think . . . it couldn't?'

'It's possible. You know it could happen. Think what we could do.'

The two hunched on the counterpane trying to remember what things would bring on a period. Hope pinned her left eye with her hands. She thought of the tin again in the corner of her mother's desk. Joanna remembered Lavender's literature which didn't mention this. They could drink a lot of water, to make them pee. There was quinine. There was lying in a boiling bath while you drank gin. There was violence, punches the belly, falling. In old days women used knitting needles, dying of blood poison.

'I think we ought to exercise. We'll start at once. There isn't time to lie about. Come on.'

'How could I possibly be pregnant. If I were I'd feel it. It's wet out and it's Sunday. You babble about roller skating.'

'Come on Hope. We dare not risk waiting.' They must jump and bang as much as possible. Her own period was due.

The rink was near their new chalet, another derelict place with a corrugated roof that leaked. A deaf old man was in charge, looking like an undertaker. He grumbled as he showed them where to find the skates. No one realised that once he was an expert. Girls thought they could learn in half an hour and they rarely stayed long enough for him to glimpse their frillies. A few falls and they went. Wooden railings like pens were arranged in alleys for beginners. He told them to start skating there, the pens would break the falls. Hope told him they weren't cattle. Joanna said they should do what he suggested, to get the idea of wheels under their feet before they started seriously. They both felt sick. They swallowed chocolate-flavoured laxative to hurry their inner tubes along. Hope whined about her aches and didn't want to try. She leaned against the pen and watched while Joanna lurched her way to right and left. Her skates crashed against the rails, she disregarded falling. 'Watch me Hope, I'm getting the hang of it.' She got up from her back, dusting her jeans' seat, she urged Hope to come on and try it because the remedy was a challenge in itself. The old man watched them, the idle girl and the plucky one who tried and fell. He liked their bright hair. If you couldn't look at knickers hair was nice. The only way to learn was to keep at it.

Clapping hands sounded inside the entrance. A voice called 'Congratulations. That's the way to succeed. You're plucky.'

The old man brightened. John was the only entertainer who bothered about him. John took the trouble to visit him, he came daily to shout into his deaf ear and drink tea. It was John who saw he got his pay packet. He yelled out that he had the kettle on for him, to come on over.

'Hullo John, I saw you on the trampoline,' Hope said. Yesterday was another existence. The sight of John revitalised her.

'You did? I saw you in the ballroom. I remember you. Are you alright? I worried about what has happened.'

Hope turned to watch Joanna by the railings. She wanted no mention of disaster. Handsome John remembered her. He'd noticed. 'This is my sister Jo. I'm Hope.' She grasped his sleeve childishly, she wanted to hold him. He asked her if she was fond of sport. She made him feel like Hercules. Joanna said with firmness that they'd come to the Camp for the sake of the sea air. Hope's lighted face filled her with foreboding. Hope was man-mad. John looked as if he'd like to swallow her. Unaccountably she thought of the foolish face of Euphemia reciting rhymes, as Hope explained to John that she'd like to learn, was terrified of falling. John, overjoyed to find her, alive and pale on roller skates, said that he'd teach her. He'd come for a word with the old man who depended on him, was ready then to give her instruction. Teaching was his vocation.

He went to shout into the old man's ear about the fair worker who had been lost that morning early. The old man was only interested in tea, his pay packet and Campers' frillies. A death was not his affair.

Hope clunked her skates impatiently. When John rejoined her he wore special racing skates with wheels that spun. He kneeled to check that Hope's were properly strapped. He took some chewing gum from his pocket. 'Have some', he said, unwrapping the flattened stick, putting it on her tongue like a sacred wafer. She felt caught up, infatuated. He'd chosen her. 'Now Hope, take my hands.'

He walked her to the rink, shifting his grip so that their two hands crossed safely. 'Don't stiffen, I will guide you. I'm not letting you fall.'

'Promise?'

'I said so. Trust me.'

97

He drew her swiftly. The smell of peppermint was like a breeze on her throat. The swiftness surpassed the thrill of the roundabout or fascination of watching him tumble. He glided her in forceful swoops from side to side, leaning towards the centre as they cornered. He'd come to save. He'd straighten out her life. She loved mint.

'Joanna, look. I'm skating. I haven't fallen at all. Look.'

Joanna didn't answer. In the days on the farm, playing in the meadow, or in their home in Putney she'd not envisaged being parted, had assumed their lives would always intertwine. She heard Hope say that her young sister was an onlooker by choice, a solitary person who didn't mix easily. She wanted to know about his life, and if he liked the Camp.

'I'm here for the season. It's an experience. I wouldn't want to come often.'

'What work do you do?'

'I teach. In Dublin. I teach English.'

'I didn't think you were Irish.'

'I am.' Normally reticent about himself he felt he wanted to explain his ideals to the beautiful intelligent and friendly girl. As though the pattern of his summer had changed he wanted to confide. He loved his country and was patriotic, now they'd met he no longer regretted coming to the Camp. He liked the way the sisters stayed together. He put loyalty before anything.

Apart from the conductor who'd said 'your majesty' she couldn't think of any other Irishmen. He had beautiful teeth, evenly cream. His hair was neat above his polo neck. They leaned against the rail the other end of the rink and he kept his arm round her in case her skates slipped. He wanted to know how she was feeling about the death. He didn't mean to pry or to upset her, obviously she'd had a shock.

'It's just that I don't want to talk about that. Not now.'

'As you wish. Do you want to rest?'

'Shall we go round again? Tell me about Ireland. They worship the Pope and Mary. Tell me.'

'It isn't quite like that. Non-catholics get confused. The dogma is complicated.'

'You're not married?'

'Not yet, no. I've been teaching for three years. Originally I came from the North.'

'Where the troubles are? I wouldn't like a country where there's fighting.'

His country's plight saddened him, but he wouldn't want to leave. The atmosphere in the Camp was limited, stultifying, crazy too. Discovering her there was wonderful, a bonus.

Joanna hobbled in her skates to the locker room. The old man resented the girls now, they'd taken John's attention away from him. He muttered to Joanna that he'd known the fairground chap was a wrong'un, the lot of them were no better than ruffians. As he spoke she tripped on a bit of loose mat and fell over again, hearing the seat of her jeans rending as she hit his matting. The old man grinned, a sight of knicker crutch at last, his patience was rewarded. He said a fall like that could jar you, she should sit down and recover. She said that she had broken his skate, was sorry. Hope and John didn't see her fall and the old man didn't care. Under the teapot on his table was a folded newspaper. A notice with a box number said 'Semen donors wanted for research. Cash offered.' Men aimed their stuff into bottles for scientists to look at and got paid. They'd swilled stuff worth money from their limbs. Fortunes went down drains. The old man stared rudely at her body. 'I'm sorry about the skate', she said. 'Your skate is broken.' And she felt the pain, vee-shaped, sharp, the pain for which she worked, pain that heralded the time of month. Familiar stickiness, wet that must be looked at. Her falling in the pens, falling on the rink and now on the old man's mat, had worked the trick. She'd say goodbye to him, would leave for the pink chalet, to wipe and re-wipe herself in extreme relief. She was in the clear. There was only Hope now.

'Whatever is it now? You do make a fuss Joanna. Isn't John divine? He bought me sweets as well.' Hope sniffed her fingers, smelling the lingering peppermint. Her limbs no longer hurt. John had cured her pain and sorrow. Now it was Joanna's turn to lie on the pink bedspread and look devastated. Joanna should have stayed for longer on the rink, she would have learned not to fall.

'Look again, Hope. Make sure.'

'Why should I peer into my pants? I haven't got the curse, nor am I pregnant.' John had talked to her about his native Dublin. She'd listened, picturing it all. The money imprinted with animals, the people's odd religious habits in the home. The way they spoke so colourfully and offered strangers bits of buttered cake. They drank a lot in shops that opened late. The Dublin people were friendly and had time for you. They weren't ruled by clocks. To find Joanna still complaining was an anti-climax. There was no question of babies, she was built narrow. She and John planned to skate again. Meanwhile she felt worn out. She told Joanna to move over, make room. Joanna spied and worried and sleep-walked. Joanna was enough to put the dampers on a rainbow.

Their night in the pink chalet passed quietly. This pink section was too far away to hear the loudspeaker, except when the wind blew south. They were woken by a thumping on their door.

'Who wants us?'

The receptionist with the lacquered hair was outside with an annoyed face, 'a party came. They asked for you. I haven't time to run round after individuals. Haven't you got ears?'

The sisters discussed who it might be. Joanna bit her thumb and said they must be prepared for official quizzing. Hope said it would be their mother come to get them. Joanna's ankle pained her after that final fall. She limped.

It was not their mother or the police that paced along the edge of the swimming pool but Miss Delicate. She looked grotesque in her once saffron dress and her indestructible stockings. She wore surgical shoes that trod the concrete ramp with firmness. The shoes were new to the sisters, who were used to her raffia ones that she rotated under her desk in Putney. Miss Delicate didn't see them, she was too absorbed in the swimmer in the water. At first she'd thought he was in difficulties, had sped over the grass to his assistance. She saw that the reason for the fellow's arm-waving was his extreme thinness. His shoulders and elbows thrashed the surface like the long legs of a bird. Because of this he took his plunges early. At night or early was the time for those who didn't look their best in swim-suits. He flailed his limbs from thinness, not from drowning. He wore a cap of thin black rubber to protect his ears and Miss Delicate was so interested that she forgot her reason for coming. He looked back at her. Their astonishment was mutual.

'Miss Delicate, Miss Delicate what are you doing here?' Hope had been so sure the visitor would be their mother she felt almost cheated.

'Miss Delicate?' said Joanna unbelievingly.

'Ah Hope, and sister Joanna. I have come.'

'But why?'

Miss Delicate explained that their mother had requested her by post to find out their situation. She had been delighted to comply. She'd come down to estimate. Their mother was a busy woman. It was her pleasure and a chance of country air. 'But what's this Joanna? Limping?'

'I fell.'

'And both your faces looking long? A mercy it isn't broken. Why so wan the two of you?'

'We're alright.'

Miss Delicate said how jolly everything was, turning again to the swimmer who had swum to the edge by their feet, gripping the rope, his snout-like face touching his fingers. She'd like to be introduced.

'It's not jolly at all', Joanna said.

'You've made a chum or two?'

Lil Pratt and Co. came over the grass, drawn by curiosity. The gents were within earshot. Miss Delicate felt exhilarated. Times changed. Now there were Camps for peasantry, money invested for their gratification. Instead of hop picking in Kent, these cockneys with adenoidal expressions were lapped in luxury with students to wait on them. Their leisure was organised to fine precision. Here, mannikins were made welcome as well as the aged or emaciated. Life could be harsh, she'd never seen a family so fat, a swimmer so thin or little men so small, but here they could forget care. A week of joy and peace without responsibility was what they paid for. She'd write this in her report to Dr. Greenham. These people had liberty. She had also come because she was uneasy about Mallory.

Since the fracas she had written belatedly to check his credentials. She wrote the letter she hadn't sent before because of saving the stamp and she'd received a reply from Lady Start in East Shropshire. Spikey writing covered page after page, leaving Miss Delicate quite in the dark. Something had distressed dear Lady Start to the point of illegibility. 'Of course the lad . . . I remember the name . . . Mallory. The shindy . . . thirty years ago . . . reluctant to recall . . . Stable hand . . . ostlers given to carousing . . . wallow in their cups . . . Sir Oswald (R.I.P) was unaware . . . Criminal activity . . . injury to the mare

101

(R.I.P) Sir Oswald reluctant to prosecute . . . Mare unable . . . E. Shropshire flatrace . . . lad fired. Pained and reluctant to recall.' Miss Delicate was quite befogged. Mallory had been guilty of something unpleasant with regard to a dobbin, was unsuited to have the charge of Hope. She'd posted this mysterious letter to the Camp. She wished no ill to a living soul, but persons with records of equestrian misbehaviour were better employed out of reach of people, particularly young girls. Street-tidying, scaring birds from crops would be more suitable. She thought the Camp should see the letter.

The sight of the girls uplifted her. She would be able to reassure the doctor with entire truth. The good lady could pursue her valuable work in the prevention of birth with a quiet mind. She'd find out all she could about these peasants before she went, watch how they made merry. Mallory had placed Hope in comfort. It seemed to her the Campers all got treated royally. She was pleased that she'd decorated her hat with poppies, adding some corn ears. She held her brolly like a crook.

'Joanna do I see signs of recent tears?' The girl was red about the eyes.

Lil and brood stepped closer, the gents forgot their ruling not to eavesdrop openly. This lady was beyond credence, Duchess perhaps, some close relative of their lady girls. The receptionist looked through the window by her desk. The old lady made a show. The flashlight chappie unstrapped his camera. The swimmer had the ringside view. He compared the woman to a lady Frankenstein or someone from a Hammer film. Lil Pratt forgot to fill her mouth. Her lips hung wet and slack and open. She'd not seen a titfer like that since the film of mountain people in the Dardanelles, made after World War one. The Super checked the programme. No activity was listed by the swimming pool so early. Unplanned events were not encouraged. The dawn suicide the day before had made a lot of work and worry, had banjaxed things for a while. He had to be extra vigilant.

'Introduce me', cried Miss Delicate. This crowd was big enough for dancing. A shepherd's hay was simple. The fat mother and her young, the good fellow hiding his bones under the water, the man with his camera and those men in blazers could make a set. She'd teach them.

The gents held their hands high to shake the Duchess. Their spiritual bond with the girls entitled them to be first. Her large old hands were cold.

'I'm Lilian Pratt. This here's my kiddies. Pleased I'm sure.'

'I'm bucked myself', said Miss Delicate. She prided herself on her ability to mix. The flashlight chappie snapped his box. The water lapped round the swimmer's head with a hollow sound. Miss Delicate suggested that they sit down. The grass was comfortable. They all grouped round her on the soft green, for once not concerned with doing what the programme said, for once forgetting that their mouths weren't eating.

'Now children tell me what is wrong. Hope, where is your paramour?'

Joanna started gulping first. She cried not so much for anyone's death as for shame at Miss Delicate's peculiar clothes, and the fact that once she'd adored her. 'He's dead', she said.

'Yesterday. He hung himself', said Hope, keeping her eyes wide and still. She must keep serene and lovely for John.

'Dead? What bosh. He can't be.'

'It's true though', Hope said. There was the prospect of skating later with John again. Though true and frightful the death was a bonus.

'It must have been his brain disturbed', Lil said, her breath catching. 'I thought the world of Ed.'

'Excellent fellow, he laboured in the pursuit of others' pleasure.'

'Oh quite.' The gents' mouths began to quiver and to droop. The swimmer slopped the water round his elbows.

Miss Delicate produced a hanky like a flag from her reticule. It was dumbfounding, somehow they must adjust. Their tears must be staunched. The fates had sent her to teach them that sorrow was enriching, nobling. The fates knew best. They needed her.

103

9

Miss Delicate liked the pink chalet. Nice and quiet. She had a look at the programme and noticed an entire lack of intellectual pursuit. A Camper's day consisted of bingo, racing, eating. All dancing was of a vulgar kind and nothing was calculated to uplift the mind. She wished she'd brought along percussion instruments, some poetry or sheet music. They needed art. What they did not need was all those gambling machines and rudeness. Their eyes needed to look on beauty, their lips to blow and carol instead of eat. When she arrived at reception the lady with a beehive hairstyle had said 'If you've come for the tall girl with the accent she's gone to the Pinks with her sister. Far corner.' Miss Delicate thought the girl was of unsound mind. The camp needed someone enlightened to show the way.

'I shall not forget the weeping of those mannikins. I believe they weep from boredom.' She rubbed Joanna's ankle as she spoke. She hung her brolly over the mirror. Their programme lacked a great deal.

'I've made friends with a man who teaches sport, Miss Delicate. I can roller skate now', Hope said, still sniffing. She checked in the mirror to ensure that sorrow kept her face gorgeous.

'This ankle is red. Swollen too', Miss Delicate said, rubbing the bone. Tending the poor ankle, listening to the tale was a new kind of fulfillment. She had Lady Start to thank, and her dobbin dead from some tomfoolery. It was almost too much to take in. Bereavements, mannikins, ankles, classes for the camp and lovers gone to grass. She surged with enthusiasm.

Joanna felt languid. The pink chalet was a shadow of the practice room. She was in the charge of Miss Delicate again. For the moment she could forget worrying about Hope. Hope would always need and love her. Anything else was unthinkable.

'He is ambitious Miss Delicate. He teaches English in an Irish school.' He loved his country, would go far. His own school was his

104

goal. It was important that Miss Delicate understood that she was an adult now, and fancied by a graduate.

Further down the row of chalets the gents congratulated themselves that the lady girls were in their part, and the Duchess. They took extra pains with their appearance for Monday dinner. The pink section was discrimating about the right inmates.

The lacquered-haired receptionist knew the value of a still tongue. She'd handled mail for years. Camp references were her department. She'd opened Lady Start's letter from East Shropshire, guessed what she was on about. 'Reluctant to recall' meant something about sex. The mare had been interfered with in no uncertain way. Mallory and the ostlers had been larking. The mare had been done, the bugger got the push. Mud clung. Peculiar caper long ago in some stables in East Shropshire. So she'd sent for Ed Mallory late on that unlucky night. She'd said 'Look chum, does the name of Lady Start mean anything? I'm broad-minded see, but just you watch it. I've got your number.' She'd spoken plainly, then torn the letter up. Least said soon forgotten. She had not been surprised to hear about the stiff in the Lads. A dark horse would try any trick. Rotten ending though.

Lil Pratt's holiday had taken an upward turn since the arrival of Miss Delicate. The week fizzed with surprises.

'Well Missus, honoured. Please to sit with.'

'Mrs. Platt, how pleasant. The air has given me an appetite.'

'Pratt dear, Pratt. Your Hope would be in a right pickle but for me. I've given an eye to Ho. And Jo. I took them in, in a manner of speaking.'

'How kind.'

'Come for your holiday? You heard the news? That poor man and his watch, just think. Diabolical.'

'I'm head of Hoaley. The girls attend there, or did until recently.'

'Lovely. What class of work is it you do?'

'I am head. Owner head of Hoaley Academy for many years.'

'Quite nice too. Funny but I'd put you down as having something to do with letters. Postal sorter is how I'd class you.'

'I handle missives. I have had no experience of post offices.'

'Learning is wonderful. I always say that learning is the basis of all knowledge.'

'What would you say Mrs. Platt to something fresh, to fulfill and stretch your horizon?'

Lil said she was quite happy with her kiddies, had never felt the lack of learning. The lady wasn't married then? Miss Delicate said that physically, in the literal sense she was unmarried. She chumped her jaws appreciatively on roast potatoes.

'Not physical? What's wedlock if it isn't physical? To have a kid is what a woman's for. What's wedlock if it isn't for a kiddy? Not that I am free and easy. My kiddies all have their Daddies. My Herb belongs to Jim. I'm not permissive. No offence to you, Ho.'

'Speak for yourself, Lil. I don't believe in kids. I don't plan on having a single one.'

Miss Delicate said that marriage was a worthwhile state for those not chosen to the world of art. Lil asked her to explain what she meant. She looked baffled when Miss Delicate asked her if she or any of her flock would take part in poetry or wind instruments. Herb made a rude sound. Lil looked further at sea when Miss Delicate spoke of madrigals and explained her dancing method. The youth of England could dance their way to knowledge by their self-formed alphabet. Lil wanted to deal with the subject of Ed, Miss Delicate was intent on discussion of culture. Whatever happened it must not get about that Mallory had been known to her, employed at Hoaley. She hoped he had been honourably disposed of. The place was efficient, evil though its programme was, trading on blockishness. She'd like a word with the Commandant about it, explain her own new methods. A choir perhaps, some French, her imagination rioted. She thanked the fates the death hadn't happened in her boiler-room. With the two sisters to help her the Camp could be revitalised.

'As I was saying, Mrs. Hoaley, you knew the chap, Ed, what died?'

'I saw ... I did see him, yes.' Miss Delicate removed a shred of gristle from one of her molars. Prurience must be ignored. Mrs. Platt cried out for culture, not calumny.

'Working the whirligigs one minute, curtains next. Ever such a lovely fellow. The entertainers are keeping very mum about it, but I know better. I know he left a note.'

Miss Delicate's jaws forgot to masticate, her large hands stayed still. The girls, enjoying a meal for the first time in days put down their knives and forks. 'What?'

'He left a note before he bloody snuffed it.'

'What note Lil? Who told you? How did you hear?'

'If there is more to the affair than has been so far established, it would surely be prudent to let the matter lie.' Miss Delicate felt nervous suddenly. A note from a hand now dead could have disquieting results.

'The midges. They say that the midges know more than they let on. Some say the midges are psychic', Lil's lashless eyes popped.

'Midges? What midges?' Miss Delicate's mental signpost pointed all of a sudden to Putney, fast.

'The little gents, of course. They say they can tell fortunes.'

The sisters leaned, faces hidden, their hair hanging over their plates as the rumour was whispered round the Diner that the corpse had left a letter.

It happened as the gents left the pool, after sitting with Miss Delicate on the green grass. Auntie Bow-wow stopped them. She had a secret, she knew she could rely on them, they were old-timers. A note had been found on the cistern by the body, a scrap of torn paper. So far the writing was unreadable, that was the aggravating thing. The Commandant would be able to decipher it, the message that looked like drunken scribbling. The Super made out 'Dear D . . . yours E.M.' The gents felt this was another hour of glory, Aunt Bow trusted them. They knew a top secret. It was as good as a message from the other side. They sat at their table in the corner, quiet and proud and straight. They speculated quietly as to what the note said and nibbled at the stalks of their cauliflower portions. Their top front teeth were edged with gold.

Less food was consumed at the meal as Campers spread the word. The doubt about the passing of the fairground fellow was quite worrying. Had he been done in by another, the victim of a vendetta? Which of the two sisters had he been after? Was the lady with the brolly in the plot? Padre Shake had been seen hurrying about, his mouth set in an unpleasant line. A Camper from the Isle of Dogs said that witches' curses went in threes. Food poisoning was not ruled out. That ministrone yesterday was definitely off. A child had seen a rat round the kitchen quarters. Bubonic plague could come from a rat. The thin swimmer talked loudly. The old lady was a nutter, the girls no better, he knew them well. Three nutters, the Camp would be the better if they scarpered. Five hundred Campers whispering and the thin swimmer holding forth sounded like the breathing and shifting of a stable of beasts.

'Come then girls. We'll have another breath of ozone before I take the train back to Putney.'

'To Putney? But you've only just arrived. You're staying.' Joanna's ankle throbbed again. Hope pushed away her plate of food. She had been eating chips and cauliflower until this note affair.

'I must return. I'm needed back at Hoaley.' She bitterly regretted ever writing to Lady Start. But for her letter she'd be serenely guiding her school-girls in London.

'Don't go Miss Delicate. Everything is much nicer if you're here. I want you to meet John, the man I told you about.'

'Madame needs me. She babbles about flying, as you know she finds life a strain. She isn't young.'

'She has Major.'

'Major has his failings', said Miss Delicate darkly. Euphemia's father had complained about Major, who had been getting the kings of England mixed with race horses.

'Oh stay Miss Delicate. Stay.'

'Well, deario, I wouldn't mind a sight of the A.B.C. dancing you was speaking of.'

Miss Delicate felt touched. Already she had sowed a seed of enlightenment. Mrs. Platt would soon be clamorous. Alas, she had to leave. She suggested that they all look round the Camp, Lilian Platt, the manikins and the fat children, the swimmer too. She said she hadn't visited a fun-fair since she was a girl. It had been Epsom Downs where she had seen the animal trainer.

'No, Miss Delicate, not the roundabout, not that. We mustn't go there.'

'You shouldn't. Don't', wailed Joanna.

'An unfortunate choice of stamping-ground.'

'Oh quite.'

'I shouldn't, deario.'

'Ha ha ha.' The thin swimmer rubbed his knuckles.

They couldn't stop the progress of the stout surgical shoes into the enclosure. They watched her kick a bloomered leg.

'Help me someone, help me up. Such magnificient horses should not stand idle.' A whirl round before she took the train.

'It's fast. Hold tight', called the swimmer.

The gents began to tremble. The swimmer cheered. He'd not seen the like of those bloomers since Chiswick Empire closed.

The machine got up speed. Miss Delicate bowed to the little crowd, at her own dear girls, at the Platts, the swimmer and the manikins. Other good peasants collected to watch her ride. She swung her ferrule at them. To horse, to horse. This was her tribute, a requiem ride in honour of one who was no longer with them. Wildly sad, they must pay homage. Good Mallory involved with dobbins had made this riding possible. Ride, good Mallory, ride to happier hunting grounds and may the fates receive you. Faster, faster, let the world of art go hang, this was real living.

She heard their screams before she felt the pain; the screams of Hope, Joanna, the Pratts, the manikins and swimmer. Pain like hot liquid shot across her face, pain jarred her bones and wrenched her. Pain inside her, pulling, dragging, bumping. Black pain, blackness, falling, darkness.

*　　*　　*

There was something spooky about an old lady dragged into the centre of a circle of hobby horses, her umbrella over her face. They blamed the gamp. They blamed her surgical shoes catching in her stirrups. They said she hadn't held on tight, been careless, had a giddy turn. Two accidents in two days was uncanny. The girls had brought disaster. The gents had pointed the bone. It was the limit.

John the Sports had come out of it best. A decent chap, natural leader, it had been pleasure to obey him. 'Let there be no panic, stand back there.'

He told the elder girl to fetch the doctor, the younger to fetch blankets from the nearest bed. From Dublin, yet they trusted him. This was no Irish trouble-maker, this was directorship of the kind they admired. He set a pattern. Auntie Bow-wow lead her puppies somewhere less adventurous. Birdie, Bert, the Dining Super followed, cajoling the people away from John, bending over the torso of the old lady. They were keen to provide more cheerful entertainment

109

than the sight of someone lying in an almost perfect circle like an O. Blood from her umbrella clung in purple beads on her hair and face.

'You're having a lively week of it', the receptionist said to Hope. She rang for Dr. Bale.

'What next John? What can I do?' Hope said, panting from running.

'You sent for Bale? Good kid.'

The ambulance arrived. Dr. Bale looked pessimistic. She was lifted onto canvas stretched on poles. They closed the doors.

'My darling. Ah my love', John said, putting his arms round Hope. He led the two girls to the pink chalet.

The loudspeaker requested Camp staff to assemble in reception. The Commandant, a shy man, usually pinned his messages to the board. It was thought to be a mark of his greatness that no one had seen him. That day he spoke from a tape recorder on the Super's desk. 'Look, Staff, this is serious. There are getting to be too many accidents. You must stay in control. You must watch Campers. Stick to programme and you won't go wrong. Next season's bookings and our jobs depend on it. Stay in control, entertain with more zest. Discourage unplanned grouping, discourage whispering and long faces. Keep Campers on the move, keep them dancing, eating or playing a game of sport. Bingo for the elderly or the handicapped, got it Staff? Oh, and Staff, the old lady will live. She will recover, thanks to Dr. Bale.'

The Padre spoke to them too. There would be a thanksgiving for the lady Mrs. Hoaley, living still in spite of odds. She was lying badly bashed in the Pinks. He, too, stressed the importance of the Programme. He would wake them in the morning with a song of his own composition. The Super said that he relied on them all to a chap. Extra grub and champers for those called to work overtime due to the bother in the fun-fair. That part would be cordoned off. Had it been possible he would have got Bale to drug the rations, let everyone cool down.

'I'll never rest again', said Joanna, having swallowed the doctor's soothing pill.

'Speak for yourself. The Delicate's all right, or will be. It will take time, but she's only a few doors away, stop dramatising. I'm knackered.'

The pill that brought instant sleep to Hope did nothing for Joanna. Her life was spent in keeping watch, hot and rigid while Hope slept. She wasn't alarmed to see the handle of the door turn. She guessed it would be the gents.

They told her that her guardian would live. That Padre Shake had visited her, had talked. In passing they had heard him praying with her.

'She isn't our guardian, you know.'

'If she is not, pray who then is?'

They held Joanna's hands while she explained that Miss Delicate was in some ways more precious than a parent, since she cared about them. Careful not to sit on her feet they questioned. Where was the natural mother? What kind of person to let her daughters play fast and loose on the coast? 'Get in touch with her my little dear, the touch of a mother's hand is what you need.'

'Oh quite.'

'And correspond with her. Letters are a boon when in a fix. Accept the hand of fortune. Write to her.'

'I'm not so sure they are a boon. Letters have caused a lot of trouble. Miss Delicate might be well if it were not for hearing about a note.'

The gents twitched with excitement. They'd meant to keep Aunt Bow-wow's trust. They must have been overheard. The thought that they might be responsible for an accident made them feel divinely powerful, as omniscient as the Commandant. They went on patting her and looked about the girl's room. Hope slept on. They noticed Joanna's recorder, so brown and shiny. They discussed soothing humdrum things. They asked her if she liked dancing and was fond of sweets.

'You see, I've always wanted to be like Hope. She gets her way. Men fall for her. You can see why. Look, she's beautiful.'

'Yes, wonderful. Bestowed with pulchritude from birth. And you, my little dear, are like her mirror.'

'A looker just like you.'

They looked at Hope asleep. They watched her breathing. They leaned over, they smelled faint peppermint on her breath. The gents stretched their hands to touch her hair, a chance to touch and feel a

111

lady girl. They touched her where they thought she wouldn't feel it, feeling a thrilling power. Now all four of them were amigos.

They snatched their hands back instantly when Joanna said they shouldn't, that they should let Hope sleep in peace. They sidled out.

Joanna felt the burden of Hope's future. She was tired of responsibility. She decided to confide in Lil. She left Hope sleeping like a dead person and recrossed the Camp. The steps rattled again as she ascended. She rapped at Lil's blue door, not looking at the one next door where she and Hope had spent the first night.

Lil and her family were turning in early. Worn out by excitement they could take no more. Their chalet smelled of singed hair while Lil used the curling tongs. Each child waited to have their curls tightened.

'So you see Lil, I can't help being worried. Not that she's late or anything, but I worry. Look out Lil, you'll burn Herb's head.'

Lil looked at the curl stuck to her tongs over the head of Herb. A smoking, fizzling shred came away. 'You mean to say she never took precautions?'

'I told you nothing is certain yet. Not yet.'

'It's certain, don't you kid yourself. I should know, shouldn't I? Whatever was your mother thinking of?'

'She's busy. Our mother is a busy woman.'

'Busy doing what? I thought her work was in that line?'

'It is.' Their mother's patients would laugh her out of Putney if it happened.

'You hippy lot. I do not bloody understand. I take a risk, I know what I am doing. I have a kid each year, that's what I like. Having it up is for a kid. You hippy lot you don't want them, yet you bloody act as if you did. What sense is that?'

'What can she do Lil? Please help.'

'There's nothing. Pills will only give her the runs. I don't hold with that abortion lark, it's weakening. Lot of nosy parkers, they want your life story plus what you had for dinner. Who is Hope's fella?'

'I . . . I think it was . . . Ed.'

'Poor bleeder, guessed it might be. He's off the map at any rate. There's nothing she can do bar surgery.'

'But Lil, we want to keep it quiet.'

112

'It isn't you that's up the pole by any chance? Why don't she come herself to me? I took her in.'

Lil's mouth glistened stickily across her face as she spoke of her child who had been lent to her. Life was unfair.

'She's too upset to speak herself.'

'She didn't look upset to me, not last night she didn't. I saw her jazzing off with John. I took her in, I treated her like one of mine. Why don't she come herself. Have I got the plague or what?'

'You're a friend Lil. I came because I knew you'd help us. Please.'

'Well, Jo, you better tell your Ma. That's my advice, to tell.'

'We can't.'

'She better marry John the Sports. I dare say that's what she'd rather. But what about yourself? Shall I touch you up with my tongs? Curls would make something of you. You don't make enough of yourself.'

10

'Exactly what's it all about? What have I done? Hope rushes off to some Camp for tourists. You go haring after her. Now you come and say she's married. Is this the thanks I get?'

'Please don't take it like that Mother. Hope's husband is nice. You'd approve of John, I'm sure. Please don't be upset.'

'But why? Why did she?'

'They just decided in a hurry. They're happy, very happy.' Happy alone, happy in their love, happy in their kisses, their embracing. Happy without her, their love sanctioned by the holy church. She needn't have consulted Lil, Hope and John couldn't wait to get married. The wedding had been as speedy as possible.

'But what does she know about him? Why the urgency?'

'She just wanted to get married. Some girls do. Hope is romantic. I thought she ought to wait.'

Joanna watched her mother fiddling with her cactus plants. She felt little pity for her, though her hornrims enlarged the bewilderment in her eyes. She brushed the spines with the tips of her fingers. Sensitive doctor's hands more tender with plants than with her children, more interested. She told her that she had wanted Hope to write about the marriage, that they tried to telephone, had got no reply.

'Am I supposed to thank you for your consideration? That you thought about me?'

'I begged her to be sure about it.' She had begged her with a frantic face. 'Think twice', she'd said. Happy marriages were rare, they themselves were proof of one that failed. Hope had only smiled. She was sleek from the love and touch of John and she had spoken of wedding dresses. She had told Joanna that she must walk behind her. Not a bridesmaid, it was informal. Joanna was to be the Lady in Waiting. Joanna must stop making objections and help her to pack. She and John were to fly to Dublin directly after the service. She had given Joanna a small black string horse. Joanna had been repulsed.

114

Hope explained that John had helped to dispose of Mallory's things, had found the black horse, unfinished, in a drawer. Mallory had carved Hop along it's under-belly. There were few posessions, some laundered overalls, some tools. John said that Hope should keep it. The dead should be honoured, forgiven, remembered in spite of happenings. 'So you take it, Jo. You take it back to Putney for me, that's the best. I cannot bear it. John is too charitable.' Joanna put it on Hope's piano in place of the white one. They both had mocking little teeth. She had packed Hope's things into the new cases, knowing it would be the last time. Hope was flying to a foreign country to start a life without her. She would be John's worry. Hope's future concerns would be orange juice, the crocheting of vests. She'd become a Dubliner, citizen of a sentimental city of buttermilk, religion and drunks. Her future countrymen threw petrol bombs. Her child would smell of incense.

'But why the secrecy?'

'I told her to write from Dublin. She will, she will.'

'When did it all happen? Put yourself in my position, I work like a trojan, I'm not getting any younger. You rush away. You leave a rabbit in the house. Pest. Fur gives me asthma. All you tell me is "She's happy." '

'You've never really thought about Hope and me. You've never worried about how we felt. We've been alone for years. You don't care if we're here or not. I hate it. I hate it. I hate it without Hope. I can't bear it here, you don't realise.'

'Stop dramatising. You know that my work is demanding. I can't help that, I'm forced to work long hours. I've had nothing but responsibility and expense. You chose that Hoaley place, it was expensive.'

'I only know I hate it here.' The home was clean and silent. She lived for a letter from Hope. All that mattered was the post, a letter with an Irish stamp.

'You are hysterical. Did she marry in a church?'

'Oh yes. A Catholic one.'

'Catholic? A Roman Catholic service?' Hope had married into a faith that had no allowance for divorce, one that forbade birth control. Joanna, cool and blatant, told her the shattering fact. Joanna had been the witness, the only confidante of Hope, had taken the role that should have been hers. She had been superceded, was a failed mother, excluded from her own daughter's wedding rite. Joanna was a thief as well as a slut. She was an over-emotional thief.

'Mother, it's all right. You'll hurt your fingers on those spines.'

'Spines? Ah yes.' She must stay controlled. Hands revealed tension. Hope's strange hands were what she'd noticed at her birth. This younger slut was staring, enjoying her superiority. 'And the young man, what does he do?'

'A teacher. I told you we tried to telephone.' They'd heard the bell ringing in the Putney hall and Joanna had shivered at the thought of going back alone. The Camp was like home by the time Hope married. The horror of Mallory's death blurred. Miss Delicate continued to lie bandaged in the pink chalet, with little of her showing except her sturdy feet which had escaped unharmed, her surgical shoes had saved them. At times her mind wandered. At nights she murmured in her sleep 'Show them, point the way.' Padre Shake spent time with her. He admired her bravery. They discussed ideals and methods of guidance in the long hot afternoons.

Their mother asked why the young man had been there, and what his prospects were. It was consoling that he was a professional, though Catholic. Her questioning was mechanical. She forgot to ask his name. She thought back to the time of the Christmas cake, Hope's watching eyes. 'Don't eat the cake Joanna, it's full of her saliva.' The girl had been venomous ever since, had acted ruinously, had made a clandestine marriage out of spite. Slut. She'd done her best. She'd slaved to keep them. Good riddance, let her go. She'd never cried before for anyone, she wouldn't now. She wouldn't give Joanna the satisfaction of seeing tears. Joanna had cold eyes too.

'She is barely of age. I'm her legal guardian.'

'It's done now, Mother.'

'I would have liked to see her married. She didn't think of that, I suppose.'

'She did look lovely.'

'Always a good-looking girl.'

'She wore a lovely dress.' Hope hadn't been nervous walking up in her broderie anglaise dress, flesh showing through the eyelet holes. She'd got what she wanted, she was scoring their mother off. At the last minute she stuck a sunhat on her head; of orange linen its brim was floppy, undulating. She'd got her man, desirable, a person to rely on, who would stay and care for her, though her pregnancy had been induced by someone else. John and sexual love had come into her life to take over where Ed had left off. Ed, dead, had wet her bed, and altered their lives. Joanna got the string horse as memento. Hope's flowers had been a horse-shoe made of small white flowers. 'Be happy, Jo. I'm so happy, be happy too.' Her eyes were huge, oblivious of previous catastrophes, huge with a happiness undreamed of. The world must be happy because she was.

'I would like to have seen her. In church you say?' She'd never confused their minds with religious dogma, believing in self-sought truth. 'Don't eat the cake.'

'Yes. Church.' They'd walked there. Hope made her step sedately. The steps echoed in the aisle of the wooden church. The building was temporary because of funds in process of being raised. The priest had interviewed the couple previously, had said 'You know that marriage is for life' and Hope had nodded dreamily. She had looked dreamy as he intoned the solemn marriage words, her orange brim looping her face. His cassock had smelled of rabbits' medication. So the knot, quietly observed, was made tight. John said that a quiet wedding was better, lending impact to the seriousness of the step. No guests, their Camper friends had gone, it was the end of the season. Miss Delicate, still bandaged in the Pinks, had not been fit to go. the Padre would have liked to officiate, but when it came to ceremony religious sects were inviolable. After it was over, the priest stood with them in the wooden porch that overlooked some graves. Children buried their pets there. 'Here lies Rover, friend for thirteen years.' The priest liked to round a ceremony off with sociability. He spoke again of the new church building, the cost of it. The animals' graves were allowed for in the proposed building plans. He spoke again of marriage being for life because rushed ceremonies made him uneasy, especially when modified to suit an unbeliever. A bonfire blew smoke over the dogs' graves, making shapes like lamenting bodies. Soon it would be winter. The priest was another Dubliner. God's city, he said, where the living was hard. He meant the cost of things and touched again on the cost of building churches. Bills weighed on his mind. Hope had looked at her bright ring fitting uneasily over the skin at the base of her finger. The priest said he'd put her in touch with a friend who specialised in

117

instruction in the one true faith and wished them love and joy and everlasting peace. Along with Irish luck as well, when John put money in his hand for the building. The breeze blew more smoke as John kissed Hope again in the wooden porch. It had been then that Hope turned Irish. She became different, assuming a special hallowed air, like the girls wearing shawls in Irish movies who ran about on mountains sneaking bandages to wounded soldiers.

Back at the Camp the Super had provided a little wedding snack. The entertainers signed a huge card that had a picture of a meadow with a stream running under a bridge. The Commandant had left a signed programme for good luck. He'd written 'Keep Smiling' above his name. Hope gave Joanna the flowery horse-shoe and had put her arms round her. 'This is real champagne. Drink. I love it. There's absolutely nothing like champagne. Joanna hated it. Pee-water. A different life was waiting for Hope and her sparkling ring. Soon she'd be boiling huge potatoes and kneeling in a church.

'She did look lovely.' She'd tried to make her face expectant over the champagne glass, not wanted to be labelled the death's head at the feast. Champagne was supposed to release inhibitions. Hope kept kissing her moistly and carelessly. Hope had no lack of kisses now. The ones exchanged with John were clingingly prolonged, wet as peaches. 'And now listen, Jo. I don't want you coming to the station. We'll be leaving soon. I don't want to see your gloomy face staring. It's enough to make our plane crash. Go on back to the chalet.' She'd implored her to stay a little, she couldn't travel to Ireland in those eyelet holes and floppy orange brim, Hope ought to change. 'Go on back to the chalet, get packed ready for Putney. I'll write to you there, I promise. Go on back to Putney.' The chalets were nearly all empty, closed for the winter. Only her and Miss Delicate in the Pinks. And Miss Delicate had the Padre.

'And what is this news about your head mistress? Is she ill?'

'The school is closed now. Euphemia told me that they won't be opening again. Miss Delicate had a bad fall. She won't be coming back to Putney.'

'It's unfortunate.' But worse if the girls had still been attending Hoaley. She'd paid their fees until she was tired of it. Money invested should pay dividends. Miss Delicate had omitted to report any wedding. She should have been informed. Miss Delicate was a bad

118

investment. She charged extortionately and gave poor results. The two girls didn't appear educated and showed no interest in careers. Scribbling and eating sweets, playing with that rabbit, were scarcely qualifications for secure futures. Perhaps it was best that Hope had married. Joanna would probably leave. She deplored Catholicism. She believed that Hope had been fond of the teacher.

'I shall miss Miss Delicate.' Their mother didn't care which child was which. Which girl married and which was lonely. She evaded emotional responsibility, putting strangers first. Her Hypocratic oath was farce.

The gents had whispered to her before they left the Camp that there was every likelihood of Miss Delicate becoming Mrs. Shake. He spent time with her. They overheard things, by chance naturally. The gents were back in Marylebone. Lil Pratt was back in Wapping. There was comfort in remembering that they all lived in the same city. It was unlikely that letters would arrive from Marylebone or Wapping. She willed the postman to walk quickly up their street. He always had mail for their mother.

'Dear Jo. You must come. I don't like it here. One kid is bad but two is the end. Please come soon. Love Hope. How can I cope with two?'

She told her mother that she'd heard. That Hope wanted her to stay with them in Dublin. Her mother said sarcastically that she supposed there was no message for her, she was only the mother. The girl ran true to type. A selfish slut issuing orders from across the Irish Channel.

'Can I go? Can I?'

'But by all means do. Join your sister Hope.' A temporary measure that might be final. Let her go. Some women were not made for motherhood, they lacked the right vibrations. She'd tried, no one could have done more. Chalk it up as failure. She was free. In future she would lead her own life. She'd let or sell the house, go where she was needed, go where she'd receive respect. Women needed her. Sell out, forget the past and the sluts who did nothing but give annoyance and expense. No more sneering, burned pans, rabbits and locked doors. All the same she would have liked to have seen Hope married. She said that she would like to send a gift. She'd look out something for her kitchen. Because money healed rifts and Hope had once been part of her. She must have made a beautiful bride.

119

She cried when she was alone, away from Joanna's cold eyes. She put her head in the linen cupboard and they fell onto the towels. She reached for the packets of sales bargains, parcelled in celophane ready to travel across the water to Hope's kitchen. Tea cloths. She liked bargains, observed frugality, had little guessed her daughter's kitchen would be their destination when she bought them. A soap-offering to the girl who scorned her. Pretty towels to travel to the place where birth control was sin. Hope's countrymen were hooligans given to religious warfare, campaigning in public houses. No lecture hall in Dublin would welcome her, where the population was explosive. She put her head on the towels and wept because her skills would be rejected. Hope had rejected her. Somewhere she had failed them. Instead of fostering self-reliance she had fostered enmity. She cried as well because she wasn't young, was neither beautiful nor desired.

Joanna watched her write the cheque, watched her change two hundred into three, fearful of being thought mean at the last. Her mother was getting rid of two burdens. The ink spatted as she wrote the sum and signed the erasure. All that concerned her was to say goodbye, to leave and join Hope.

Her world had turned starry. She had money to buy clothes, money to travel to where Hope needed her. She bought a book on baby care, marking the chapter about twins. She bought Johnson's baby soap.

Her mother moved her desk into Hope's bedroom as soon as she heard about the marriage. Now she had a proper study until arrangements could be made about moving from the house. She left a note on the kitchen table on the morning of Joanna's departure. 'Eat a good breakfast before you go. Please write that all is well with Hope. Your loving mother.' Joanna had never received a letter from her. She had suggested that Joanna take an office course. Qualifications of any kind were advisable. It didn't do to rely on luck or others for your bread.

She booked her flight by telephone, talking down it in the Putney hall for the last time. She saw the rolling dog for the last time. Her brain felt like a sleep-walker's. She would waken in a foreign land.

'My sister, a Catholic, is having twins', she explained to the hostess who welcomed passengers onto the plane. She'd never flown before, she explained. She'd like a window seat. The hostess flashed her papist teeth and spoke with an oily brogue. She asked what part of Dublin the sister lived. A gorgeous city, gorgeous. A jiggy tune poured into the fuselage, welcoming them ahead of their arrival. Joanna's hands sweated because leaving London for good was no trifle. She put them in her pockets. A net was fixed to the seat in front, containing literature concerning God's green island, as well as bags for vomit. The bags were indestructable. She hadn't answered Euphemia's last imploring letter asking her to tea. Euphemia would have no one now. The literature showed architecture, churches mostly, and hotels with *haute cuisine.* The hostess offered round a basket containing glucose sweets to stop the ears from popping during ascent. Air-travellers were well-bred, their minds transcended tuck. Joanna worried about the fastening of her seatbelt. She worried about her luggage. She worried about her hands, in case they steamed. Other travellers had brief cases, ready for a day in Dublin spent in conducting business. She cracked her thumbs as they rose into the air, having raced at speed down convergent runways. When she was able to look out the Thames lay wriggling through a London too far below them for her to recognise the colour of the buses nose-to-tail on various bridges. The hostess told them they could undo their seat-belts. Coats were removed and brief cases opened. Above the clouds it was ghostly, with cracks of silvery blue lit by sun between sudden walls of white. The glass was thick and safe between her and the fog-white heaviness. They went on pointing upwards through the foggy white and silvery blue. Any lurching, the hostess said, was due to air pockets. Joanna wished she'd taken off her coat. It was a warm new one, suitable for an unknown country. She wore high boots and a fringed scarf that touched the ground. Coffee was served in individual pots with cream in little cartons which she managed to spill over her scarf and her neighbour's papers. In Dublin she would become competent, manage seat-belts, pour cartons cleanly, learn not to be nervous of crashing or strange men. She would learn the art of relationship. The sugar was brown crystals that made the drink delicious. The hostess flashed her teeth every time they altered height. Once over open sea it was like no man's land. Putney, the Camp and its strange people, the tragedy and Hope's love affair, were part of another world, a phantom place.

She'd expected green landscape the other side but beneath them

121

the land was greyer than London, softer looking. The grey sea edging Dublin bay was quiet against a no-colour shore. The tide was out. Ireland looked empty. No highrise flats here or factories but small groups of houses in a greyish land. And at the airport Hope was waiting, unable to manage life in the dull land without her, expecting her twins and miserable. Perhaps the same toothy hostess had attended her on her wedding flight, had strapped the seat-belt round her and handed her a sweet. The travellers were anxious to start their business day, to re-open the contents of the brief cases after having landed without a bump. Joanna's scarf caught in the toe of her boot as she rushed down the steps.

'All right don't manhandle me. People are looking at us.'

'But I'm so happy.' She felt washed with love for Hope. They were together.

'All right, just cut that out. This isn't London. Where did you get that coat?'

'*She* gave me a cheque. Part of it is for you. A present. But you're *fat*, Hope.'

'What do you expect you fool? Don't stare. Did *she* say anything about the twins?'

'No. She was upset about your marrying. Is such fatness normal?'

'Of course. Stop staring. I want to know what she said.'

'Oh nothing, I couldn't tell her. You're certain it's twins and not something wrong with you?' She'd not been prepared, had never seen such a size of stomach poking from a coat, as large as another person. You couldn't relate the Hope in broderie anglaise to this. Her jawline was less bony, her fingers puffed. She'd qualify for a peep-show.

'Shut up you fool, stop glaring at me. The Clinic told me. It's their job to know. They're highly skilled and qualified. You must realise that Dublin is different. You mustn't stare. You must keep your voice down. Your voice is loud and English.'

'In London you couldn't do enough to get noticed. What's got into you?'

'I've told you this is Dublin. I'm an Irish citizen.'

'You wanted me to come, didn't you? You said I had to.' She'd soon accept her Irishness, her size and married state. Hope wanted her. Already her accent had changed, was sing-song like the hostess on the plane.

'I knew you'd be watching the post and pining. You mustn't shout and stare, but fit in with our ways.'

'I will, I will.' She didn't need to ask if Hope was happy. Happiness shone from her. Her skin smelled exotic and lemony, her hair was bright in the cold air. Erect and vast she walked quickly through the air terminal. She wore no glove on her left hand, still proud of her glinty rings. Officials looked at her. She asked what was the medal she had round her neck.

'A medal of Our Lady. John gave it me.'

'Pregnancy must be sending you loco. Religious charms round your neck, what next? You used to say religion was an opiate, now you wear medals with saints on them.'

'Lower your voice. Dubliners don't talk of pregnancy except in hospitals. They say "on for a baby". A child is a mark of favour from heaven.'

She spoke seriously as she explained that religion was the most important thing in life, the basic essential. Joanna had almost to run to keep up with her. She was astonished at Hope's fervour. She made Joanna halt for a flock of nuns to pass, turning aside respectfully. In Putney she would have jeered at them. She used to mock church-goers. The nuns preceded them up the steps of the airport coach. They spoke with Welsh-sounding accents because they were from Cork. Travellers' eyes went soft and loving when they fell on the nuns or Hope. The men wore religious emblems in their lapels and raised their hats on passing a church. Signposts and names were written in Irish. People didn't look so serious here. The nuns took out small black books. Hope said they were reading their office. The clergy never wasted time. They sat quiet and contained with eyes down. Joanna and Hope sat at the back. Those passengers not reading missals read the contents of their brief cases. Hope's hands were half hidden by the bulge under her coat. Both enjoyed the scenery as they drove. They passed a newspaper hoarding 'Further bomb outrages. Derry girl tarred and feathered.' Hope said that the South was peace-loving, not like the North. She wanted Joanna to like Ireland, she drew her attention to a child by the road holding a hen above her head out of reach of a bounding dog. Free-range eggs and oven-ready fowls were advertised. If a nun smiled it made the recipient feel chosen.

'I wish you wouldn't turn, Hope. It's cockeyed.'

'You're barely in the country before you start objecting. I have my own life now. You know John is a Catholic and what it means to him. I will be one soon. There's only one faith.'

'They fight about it. How can it be right?'

'It's right. Our children must be brought up in the faith. Anything else would be unthinkable.'

'The place seems to be stiff with churches and priests. Are they to rule you now? Where is your own mind?' Hope had gone mealy-mouthed, speaking as if she'd learned her words by heart. She told her that a family that prayed together stayed together, that prayer was the real power. She kept smiling ingratiatingly at the nuns. Marriage had changed her more than she'd expected. She was worse than a dervish.

They passed open land in process of development. Pieces of piping lay in ditches. Bricks and sacks of mortar waited, covered by tarpaulin. Housing estates were planned, Hope said. The country was emerging. Industry would boom, the people of Ireland would prosper, though now there was evidence of poverty. She was proud of a professional husband. A teacher never lacked employment. The coach was stared at by old women in black. They stared as though modern inventions were curiosity. Children wore coats too tight under the arms. Buses and pillar boxes were green instead of red. The conductor handed them change with greyhounds and hens on it. She asked Hope if shamrock grew in the fields, if it grew wild. She asked her if she knew anyone in the North, if she knew anyone involved in the troubles.

'Don't mention troubles. John lived in Londonderry. He's sensitive.'

'Why did he leave?'

'It's got nothing to do with us down here. Don't talk about that. Wait until you see the Liffey and the lovely Georgian houses.'

Newsboys in rolled-up trousers shouted the latest racing results. Dubliners had a love of sport in the blood. Racing, bombs and the observance of religious ceremony were serious. Church bells rang in the cold air.

'Do you miss Putney at all, Hope?'

124

'There's nothing there to miss. Here I am a whole person. Wait until you see our flat.'

Hope pointed out O'Connell Street, said to be the broadest in Europe. She said the people of Dublin were so good it made her feel ashamed. They passed a shrine in the street's centre, with pink and blue flowers arranged round the base. Pedestrians looked and crossed themselves before entering shops. The G.P.O. and other monuments commemorated the country's torn past but other buildings were shoddy. The Liffey was the colour of Guinness floating with sticks and bottle-tops. The green buses lined up on the bridge, their drivers hunched, coat-collars turned up. The shoppers spoke of snow to come and snow of previous winters. Housewives conferred over filling recipes for soup and candles to keep their families warmed. Hope said the North side was invigorating though less affluent. The air was healthy there. Joanna looked politely at the women in shabby clothes and plastic earrings, who laid their infants on top of baskets containing potherbs for their stews. Prams and push-chairs were choked with small faces. Sacred Heart badges were pinned to pram-covers. Bells chimed the mid-day Angelus. You couldn't forget religion, with bells, dog collars and shrines to remind you. The cold was piercing, a damper cold than London. The grey of the streets and buildings merged with the grey of the skies. The girls' booted feet rang on the pavements of the North side where tenement houses waited to be redeveloped. They passed windows boarded up with corrugated tin and broken doors above steps where children crawled. Older children tied ropes to the broken railings and chanted Irish rhymes. The small general stores had bells attached to the doors and their windows offered reminders of Christmas. Old puddings in tin bowls, biscuits in broken boxes reduced for quick sale, along with cheap rag dolls that came with cornflake packets.

Flakes of snow began to fall as a playground gate crashed open to let out school children for lunch. The light fall powdered the hoods of their rain-coats, dissolving lightly in their hair.

'You have a lot of children in the place. I've never seen such a lot. I can't say I'm keen.' Joanna's cases were heavy. She wouldn't let Hope take them. In Putney Hope would not have offered.

'I agree with families. A lot of children keep the parents happy.'

Hope's street had more tall, terraced houses with ragged curtains behind warped window frames. Their doorframes had rows of broken green bells. The flaps of letterboxes were removed. Unwashed milk bottles stood on top steps. Through the broken letterboxes you could see broken hall floors. Hope didn't notice any squalor, she walked with her quick lumbering steps ahead of Joanna, like royalty. She had no interest in her neighbour's living conditions, she had her home and faith. Joanna felt excited. Soon they'd be there. They passed a Turf Accountant's where men in collarless shirts lurked. Each had a newspaper folded into a square and each looked narrow-eyed, set-faced. Hope didn't hear the workmen that whistled at them.

'Do you know your neighbours? Have you any friends?'

'Not really. But I know the lady in the flat below. She's kind. Mrs. Dunn.' There would be time for her to get to know them when her children started school. Hope saw herself standing and chatting in school and church doorways. Her children would go to nuns or Brothers. She would sew scapulars in their vests and teach them modesty.

'Do you have to go so fast, Hope?'

'You kept up with me in London, always tagging behind.'

It was consoling that Hope was still able to be acid, a ghost-tone of her old self. She carried no nose-bag now, her shoes were practical. A mongrel sniffed round the lowest of the white steps, its breath a puff of steam. Hope's front door had brass bell-buttons, the letterbox was clean. In the hall there was floor-covering and the sour smell of floor polish.

'Where's John? Is he upstairs?'

'He's still at school, of course. He would have come with me otherwise.' As they went up the stairs Hope said that Joyce had once lived in the street, that John revered his work. She was starting to read him herself. Irish writers were her concern now, not Lawrence, because of John. She was reading 'Dubliners'. John's school was near. Sometimes he came at lunch. When she said that her face dissolved lovingly.

The house was narrow, with three rooms on each floor. Theirs was the top flat, Hope explained, her feet clipping quickly. On each landing doors were shut. Some had small padlocks. The distempered walls were clean, except at the bottom of the final flight a small sticker

126

said 'Vote O'Regan. O'Regan is your man' by the green door that was ajar. 'Girl dear, thanks be to God you're back. Is this the sister? Holy God the spit of one another.' The lady who came towards them wore a coat so old its edges were worn bare like the pelt of an ancient animal. Hope introduced Mrs. Dunn. Mrs. Dunn was her friend who'd helped her when she came to Dublin first. Without her she would have been lost, Mrs. Dunn had explained about milk arriving and the dustmen, but she didn't want her spoiling Joanna's introduction to the flat above.

'See, Jo. This is our own front door. John made it. Ours is the only self contained one.'

At the top of the flight was an orange painted door, its upper panels set with frosted glass. It smelled new.

After the cold of the bare stairs the light and warmth inside was luxury. Inside the door an electric fire set high on the wall shone down, warming the sisters faces. Potted plants were on the table underneath, their tendrils lifted to the skylight over their heads. The walls were pale orange. Hope kicked off her boots under the table, told Joanna to do the same. The charcoal carpeting was scrubby under her soles. Hope showed her the kitchen overlooking the street. She was a proud housewife, her wooden draining board under the window was scrubbed and dried. Towels aired on a rack. There was a smell of baking. Cooking implements hung from the wall, arranged to size. It was in the kitchen that Hope showed the full degree of change. Herbs were in bottles, labelled, detailing the dishes suitable for their inclusion. Nests of bowls, cake tins, stools that fitted one in the other were all evidence of a new efficient Hope. The crockery was copper coloured. Behind the sweetness of her baking was the smell of paint and a whiff of linseed oil.

'I taught myself', she said. 'Look, cookies, raison puffs, date fancies. All good in moderation.' She replaced the cake tins.

'Fudge, Hope? Shall we be making it again?'

'Good heavens, no. Not now. Excess sugar is harmful. John says I shouldn't. The way we ate those sweets in Putney was rather immature don't you think?'

'Was it?'

'Besides, I've got to think of the teeth of the twins. They can be affected before birth you know. In here is the bathroom. John

127

sectioned it off. It's lovely having it so near. You can have cups of tea in the bath. He did it all himself.'

He had divided the living room too, to make a second bedroom. The large high-ceilinged rooms were the same pale-painted shade. There was room for Joanna's bed beside the cots of the future twins. Orange was Hope's favourite colour now. Electric fires glowed from various walls, John's handiwork was everywhere. He'd stripped the woodwork and kitchen chairs down to a natural state, before polishing with linseed oil. His desk in the living room window had a special lamp with a bendy headpiece. Reference books were in rows where he needed them, and sharpened pencils in a pewter mug. He'd drawn up a reading programme for Hope, was educating her. Ireland's history was her interest now, her writers survived time. Apart from the venetian blinds in the kitchen their curtains were lined velvet, which Hope smoothed into neat folds. Her hands kept touching, straightening.

'You've got everything. It's nice, Hope.'

'It's all I ever dreamed of. I love it. I love it because it's bright and light and spacious. I never could stand pokey boxes. It's bright, that's what I love.'

'You have no piano now.'

'I don't want one. Piano playing is in the past. That Hoaley stuff.'

The girls spoke about Putney and the Camp. They agreed that it all seemed like another world. Joanna told her about Miss Delicate who might never walk again and how she'd liked to have heard from Lil and the gents. Hope explained about the breathing exercises, designed for an easy birth of her twins. She hoovered every day and drank milk. She'd lined Joanna's chest of drawers with special paper, pinning the corners with tacks, and chosen a picture for her specially, above her bed, *La Femme qui pleure.*

'You used not to like modern stuff', Joanna said, politely thanking.

'John likes Picasso – he showed me. It's so beautiful and sad, two faces, straight and sideways, and the colouring.'

John sketched her too, accurate line drawings of Hope by the fire at the end of the day when the velvet curtains were drawn, the orange lamps lit, both warm and happy from love and Hope's cooking. John was helpful never minded chores. He looked forward to managing the twins. Winter's babies, they would stay indoors until the warmer

128

weather. She picked off the browned leaves of her plants, arranging their tendrils. Indoors, the size of her was even more awesome.

'Does John still do his gym?'

'Only English. The girls have crushes on him.'

'Don't you mind?' In Putney, Hope would have been jealous. In Dublin she only peered into her plants and laughed. She said she wouldn't want to be married to a man that others didn't admire and love. She was fortunate to see so much of him. The long holidays, the holidays of obligation. During these times he carried out improvements. They went walking in the Wicklow mountains where she picked flowers. Cow parsley was in a dried bunch in a jug for his desk. She said she never would grow fond of garden flowers, a reminder of Putney and lonely times, preferring the small ones of childish memory. She had taught herself to darn, and had a sewing box by his desk for when he did his marking in the evenings. She took pride in the neat state of their clothes. She showed Joanna the heel of a sock drawn over a darning egg, it's hole criss-crossed with wool. John took her to different churches to accustom her to various ceremonies.

'You are turning then. For certain?'

'Well naturally. I have instruction.'

They went back to the kitchen which was Hope's favourite room. The falling snow outside muffled the cries of the children playing in the street. Hope made coffee, the de-caffeinated kind, and Joanna thought about their shared bed under its orange spread. Soon John would come home and Hope would have to be shared, the sisterly spell would break, he'd run upstairs and kiss her. Joanna would be the honoured guest. They'd invited her, but she was on sufferance, didn't own the charcoal and orange home. They might ask her to leave. Hope spoke of John's family who had accepted her with open arms, that was the lucky part of it.

'I thought he came from Londonderry. You went there?'

'No, he has cousins here. He doesn't go up North, not since his parents died. They were in the thick of the trouble. Don't mention it. His home is here. His cousins live on the South side of the Liffey. It's fortunate that they like me.'

Hope left the kitchen to fetch the presents that John's cousins had given her, a rosary of mother-of-pearl and matching missal. She kept them separate, hallowed, in a drawer by her side of their large bed.

Their bedroom only had holy pictures, nothing modern. Sorrowing faces of saints looked down on the married couple. For Hope a bed was no longer a reminder of fear, pain, vodka and disaster. A bed was love and joy and peace. The rosary and missal symbolised their queer religion and their marriage bed. Hope fingered the beads. 'Blessed by the Pope, just fancy.' She touched the dangling crucifix. Mallory had fashioned string horses with love. The gents had painted eggshells with fine strokes of the brush; impermanent objects soon destroyed. Hope loved her beads.

'Do you ever think of Mallory now, Hope?'

'That's all past. Forgotten. We've talked a lot about it, of course. John and I discussed it.'

'Don't you mind about him then?'

'I used him. It was wrong, very wrong.' Mallory had been escape, a false escape that went in circles, arriving nowhere in a nowhere world. Her wonderful John had told her. She mustn't feel responsible for death. God ordained birth and death.

'You're sure you want me here? You really want me?'

'Of course we do. You're my sister. I want and need you. John says the way we lived in Putney was terrible. So aimless. Far too isolated.'

'She did her best, I suppose. Our mother. She has her own difficulties.'

'I find it hard to feel charity towards her.' The past should be absorbed and put to good account. Lessons for the future were acquired from past failure. John was her model and guide.

'You have changed a lot, Hope.'

'Oh not all that much. I'm longing to have a house of our own. I'd like a herb garden quite.'

'But it's so lovely here. You're moving, why?'

'Because we'll have a lot of children. Just think, I'll be a real live Catholic. I can't wait.'

'As long as you're sure you want me here. I could never believe in that religion.' The church had taken over Hope's free will. Hope had the church and John to cling to, would never rely on her in the same way. The coffee percolator bubbled into the copper-coloured mugs. They carried them to the window to look down at the children playing. The children stared up through the falling snow and saw the sisters with the long pale hair, like captive princesses in their room,

130

waiting for a prince to come. The girls were warm and safe. The children wore worn gymshoes as they played round dustbins with whitened lids. The window ledge was puffed whitely with snow. Joanna asked her if she'd heard from Lil. Hope said she could hardly remember Lil or her children now, that Mrs. Dunn was her truest friend. Mrs. Dunn knew a lot about being a Catholic and taught her things, though John said she was superstitious. Mrs. Dunn marked her scones with crosses, splashed holy water round her home, communed with her guardian angel. It was her grief that she was childless. She liked to bet, it was her weakness.

Hope bent into her oven, removing foil from the dishes inside. They were to have meat loaf made with spices, interesting pinches of herbs. She poked it to let the juices run, poured essence of tomato before repositioning the casserole. She said Mrs. Dunn was fond of holy pictures, that they brought luck. She liked nothing better than to get her feet under Hope's table and discuss the coming event. Mrs. Dunn said that prayer kept Ireland right; devotion to the faith made Ireland the darling of the Pope, she'd never slide away into a state of heresy. Mrs. Dunn's favourite saint was Jude. Anything was possible with St. Jude in your bag, he'd brought many a winner to the post. St. Jude had brought Hope's English sister to join them; she'd pray he'd engage her into the one true faith. The sisters heard her leave her flat below. They watched her negotiating the slippery steps, carrying an oilskin bag to make it look as though she was getting groceries. She'd call first to the Betting shop, then the church to strengthen the running hooves of her fancies by prayer. She was never seen without her old fur coat. She skirted round the dogs and dustbins. The children didn't mock her as they would had they been London children. The sisters, coffee mugs in hand, watched until she was a speck at the end of the street. John saw them before they saw him. He turned the corner, looking upwards. Their pale heads looking down the road at Mrs. Dunn reminded him of a Renoir, with the snow and orange curtains framing them. His mind snapped a mental picture. He'd remember how they looked, their watchfulness, the similarity of their heads, with hair falling straightly from off-centre partings. As he came closer he saw the apprehension of Joanna, the same look she had in the snap that Hope had taken before the wedding, when she had been Lady in Waiting.

131

'Look, that's John, he's coming', Joanna said. Now she'd find out if he really wanted her.

'He's come home early, because of you arriving.' Hope licked her upper lip. For the rest of her life she would care for her looks, so that John would go on adoring her. He was her core of existence, someone to dress for, to smell exciting for, to love and care for. She believed everything he said. She went to the orange door to kiss him.

Joanna didn't look at the greeting. Their silence was their kissing silence, Hope's mouth would be raised and opened to meet his. When they came into the kitchen he had his arm round her, a handful of her hair twined round his fist, their faces almost touching.

'How is my true-love's sister? Have you settled in? You're welcome.'

Joanna's tongue felt stiff as she repeated how lovely it was, lovely. She didn't know whether to go on standing by the window, whether she should shake hands or kiss. He touched her arm, including her. Hope's meat loaf smelled exquisite, mixed with percolating coffee. John took off his snowy scarf, shaking it into the bath. He said again that she was welcome, that Hope had been living for her arrival. He asked her if her bed was comfortable. She kept repeating 'lovely, lovely'.

'And what do you think of our city? You arrived with the first snow.'

'But I thought Londonderry was your city', she blurted.

'Dublin is John's city, I told you Jo. John settled here. He trained here too.'

'You're right, Jo. I was reared in the North. I left after my parents were killed.'

'Don't talk about that John, that's in the past.' Hope lost her loving contact when John spoke of Londonderry. His face closed, memory-saddened by the thought of his family, random casualties of a home-made bomb. She was shut out, could only imagine the bloodshed, terror and the violence. Ideological differences, belief in causes was a feature in the people's make-up. John's job was teaching truth. His pupils were Ireland's future, teaching them right thinking was a sacred duty.

He said that Dublin was known as a city of saints and scholars, that Jo would find that for herself. Talk of his northern past shamed and distressed him. He preferred not to discuss it but to concentrate on the present, sure in his religious beliefs, sure of Hope's adoration. His faith and wife were bonded in his mind, were his salvation. His return home each evening was a peak moment. He loved her with a love that overflowed to include her sister. He'd bought a welcoming present for the occasion. He knew they liked sweet things. The crystallised fruits were packed into a slatted wooden box, a miniature crate tacked by copper pins. Hope said that she ate everything now, though guided by the Clinic and John's counselling. She took a sugary lemon, scraping its shined rind with her front teeth. She'd made a pudding, too, with whipped-egg topping to mark the occasion. She wanted the meal to be perfect, stooping again to the oven. John watched her, touching her velvet smock, her hair, her fish-like hands whenever she came near him. He kissed her at stray moments, lightly, casually, not wanting to disconcert Joanna. Joanna saw the kisses, thinking of the late-night movies. Had Hope already achieved her happy ending? She had got her husband, home and expectation of her heavenly hereafter. They had no need of televisions now. Hope said their evenings were full enough, their private reality needed no addition. They read, listened to music or talked. John saw that she got a lot of rest. Extending the mind was preferable to watching trash. He poured orange juice for Hope from a crystal jug. Their fridge was the largest that Joanna had ever seen, lighting up to reveal cheeses, eggs, cold meats wrapped transparently. He said that Hope should lie down before eating. She'd missed her rest because of meeting Jo. He said they both should go, until it was time to eat. They must lie down with the sugared fruits and rest.

He turned the orange spread down for them. It made him happy to see that they were comfortable in the wide bed. He didn't consider such a task unmanly. Anything that brought comfort was right, worth doing well. He planned to leave some tracts by Joanna's bed. Nothing controversial or alarming, a pamphlet or two might plant a seed. He was quite happy to have her stay. But a family should all pull the same way, the right way.

Joanna lay stiffly in the warm clean bed that wasn't hers except by invitation. It smelled lemony like Hope. She breathed Hope's smell, feeling intrusive. John's pillow was cool, with two fine black hairs from his head across the frill of it. The sisters regarded each other with large eyes. Holy pictures hung on the walls about them, John's

133

rosary of wooden beads was round the lampshade. There was a copy of Aquinas' *Sumna Theologica*. So many religious objects made the bed as holy as a church.

'I don't go for all this religious business, Hope.'

'You'll get used to it. I'm so relieved you came, Jo. I get nervous. At times I'm almost sick with fright.'

'Of what?'

'Of having twins.'

Joanna told her it would be alright now, she was there. And she knew that Hope had not changed basically. In spite of John, motherhood approaching, the flat with the religious trappings and Hope's new domesticity, she was still necessary.

11

'That horse owed me money', Mrs. Dunn said sadly. She looked down at the betting stub on Hope's kitchen table. Her oilskin bag was full of them. Because of horses losing, horses letting her down, she never got a new coat, the coat of her dreams, a coat like the English sisters in the top flat. A coat of soft camel hair was what she dreamed of. Because of the horses she never got a radio, no power point or water heater. The flat upstairs was a contrast. She loved to visit and sip tea and eat the cakes surrounded by warmth and pale walls. Orange was her favourite shade. Her own baking failed her as well as the horses. She kept cheerful, her religion and her talkative nature saw to that. But when a particular horse lost it cut her deep inside. She sat looking at the ticket, her sad old face framed in her collar which had crumbs on it. Another source of melancholy was her childlessness. Mr. Dunn was dead this long while, she would have liked to have given him a child. A child would be companionable, a little child to bake for. A bet made her feel less lonesome. A few substantial wins would set her up entirely, would be a compensation for failed cakes and childlessness. She'd love to do her flat up.

'Why bother backing animals, Mrs. Dunn?' Joanna asked. Silly to invest in anything so transitory; the excitement while they ran, then disappointment. Mrs. Dunn said she'd always liked a little bet, it added relish. It did no one any harm, she stood to benefit, what was there wrong about it?

'It's boring, that's what's wrong', Hope said.

'Money ought to be earned, acquired with effort', said Joanna. She was having typing lessons three afternoons a week, was learning a skill so that she could pay her way. Mrs. Dunn should keep account of all money passed over the bookie's counter, keep track of her outlay. Hope said she wasn't saying it was sinful, Mrs. Dunn must not think that. She didn't want to offend her, Mrs. Dunn had showed her kindness. With Joanna there she was less dependent on her. Mrs.

Dunn was going shopping with the sisters. She knew where to find bargains.

The snow fell freshly every night, melting a little in the afternoons. There'd never been a winter like it. The sun forgot to shine, the snow became a topic for speculation. Mrs. Dunn said it was a sign of Heaven's displeasure at the state of the country. Worse, Irish race meetings had to be cancelled. The children couldn't play their hopping games on ice-encrusted snow. The making of snowballs became impossible due to frost. Whatever the weather Moore Street was the place for bargain poultry and vegetables. Dublin's poor collected round the stalls set up in the road. Here you could buy shell-fish, whelks and mussels in iced clusters in basins. Fowls that claimed to be fresh-killed stretched flabby yellow claws like curled hands. The market workers went to pains to make their wares alluring. A woman spat on an imported tomato before rubbing it on her coat to top the high red cone of them. Shawls were worn to keep the snow out, slung so that a baby could be contained, and a bottle of stout perhaps. Faces wrinkled early. Legs were bare and chapped. They didn't ask a lot from life. Fate was not questioned. You got married, you had a lot of children who stayed with you till they went to school. A child must do its share down Moore Street. It didn't do to rely on a man's wages. Wages had a habit of evaporating before they reached the housekeeping purse, you had to be fly to make a shilling do the work of a pound. 'Shilling a pound the tomatoes' they called. Down Moore Street there was solidarity, you were among friends. Dogs and cats had a place, keeping the gutters free of fish tails, rats or busted egg-yolks. Babies too large for the shawl lolled in handmade go-carts, an easy target for gastro-enteritis, which took its toll each year. Cold weather didn't kill germs, you learned to accept it, God's will, the hand of fate. You had a lot, you lost a couple to the angels. Candles round a coffin, following the hearse were part of life, like weather and the cost of things. A mother had a right to a nip from the bottle, a little bet, for heaven was hard. The price of things, the bitter cold, the man who came home footless on a pay day, the price, the cost of things, it all came back to that, the price of wedded bliss. Snow was bad luck, a curse, fruit rotted, green vegetables turned black, and carrots softened. Mrs. Dunn was known to them. Years back she'd had a stall herself for radishes and scallions. She was still one of them

136

at heart, though heaven hadn't blessed her with a family and she lived in idle retirement. Joanna said that surely the mothers could do better, she'd never seen such poverty, yet they smoked and nipped from bottles. Mrs. Dunn said the hungry poor must have enjoyment, the creatures were after doing their best. Snow didn't take away the smell of hens' guts. She was thankful to have gone up in the world herself.

'Trust you to run them down, Joanna. These mothers are superb.' Hope looked at one arranging kippers with chapped fingers. Ice from the kippers shone in the freezing air. These women were her people. The thought filled her with pride and a desire to be accepted, liked by them. Joanna had no understanding, these were the salt of Ireland. She imagined herself arranging fish, humble, unpacking bananas ruined by snow, a child in her shawl, a prayer on her lips.

'I'm not saying it is wrong of Mrs. Dunn, she hasn't any children. I don't think kids should be neglected.' Though the women didn't seem despondent. The street rang with their cries. 'Shilling a pound the tomatoes. Ripe tomatoes going cheap.' 'I had my money on Dirty Angel to win.' 'Hens is cheap, you won't find cheaper.' 'Take the baby from out of the fish and let the lady look.' 'Ah Bridie will we have a jar later?' Mrs. Dunn said again they knew she wanted children, but with Mr. Dunn dead this twenty year the prospect wasn't likely. She was glad Hope liked and approved her old friends, poor and dirty though they might be, with fish-scales clinging to their ankles.

'They seem to know you well here', Joanna said.

'Don't mind them, don't be noticing their blarney', Mrs. Dunn said. She informed them that she'd housekept for a family in Fitzroy Square when in her younger days. It was grand for her to revisit her old stamping ground in company with these English sisters. The Moore Street women stared as if she walked with angels. They stared at Hope's finger with the ring on it and at Joanna who wore none. They stared at Hope's belly. Twins were a mark of favour from the saints. Though Mrs. Dunn was not charmed by even numbers herself. Triplets now, there was a lucky number. They stared at the chicken Hope had bought, and listened as she spoke of herbs. She explained the use of fennel. The Irish were unimaginative where seasoning was concerned.

'A hen is grand. A grand boiler for his dinner. Fennel you say? But

why not buy your man black pudding? Black pudding does be grand
for strengthening a man. I gave Mr. Dunn black pudding every night.
Black pudding and cocoa made Mr. Dunn the man he was.'

'What is black pudding composed of? No doubt you're right Mrs.
Dunn. But my chicken casserole is superb.'

' 'Tis the animal's blood and a grain of barley. Beautiful. Ah the
lovely tomatoes.'

'Shilling a pound the tomatoes.'

'Hens is cheap the day.'

'God's curse on Dirty Angel.'

12

Hope said that John's cousins were anxious to meet Joanna.

They were at the table. Joanna looked into her porridge where the grains of demerara sugar melted into crystal pools. The cousins might be like the girls at Hoaley, mocking her in a hoard. She stirred the crystals into the grey of the porridge. The dish was novelty for the sisters, for John it was reminder of a childhood when he'd been secure, before the troubles. There was no talk of vegetarianism or healthfoods in Dublin. Hope was applying herself to quality cooking. She scoured her pans with laminated interiors, took pride in scrubbing her wooden spoon silk-smooth. Now she rested a lot and found the vacuuming too heavy. Cleaning the flat together was enjoyable. Joanna hoped the cousins wouldn't try and convert her. She'd avoided the tract left by her bed, printed by the Catholic Truth Society. Influence and guidance was to be resisted, as with her mother's family planning leaflets.

John left the tract, giving the matter into God's hands. Conversion was never wrought by coercion; example was the greatest teacher, combined with prayer. He couldn't function without faith, found it extraordinary that others, like Joanna, were indifferent. His faith in his church had never weakened. He believed that Joanna would copy Hope, given time. He'd made a bookshelf for her by her bed, provided typing paper, a dictionary and a manual of instruction. He'd lent his own machine. The kitchen table was firm and suitable for practice. The twins' room where she slept was well-lit. Their cots were ready for occupancy, painted the same pale shade of the walls. Once they arrived he thought they'd be the happiest top flat in the city. Joanna would be invaluable. Twins could be tiring. He loved to hear Hope laughing with Joanna. He was energized by the joy of guiding both of them.

His cousins loved Hope, they'd love Joanna too. He said he'd arrange a visit. He'd phone from the box on the corner.

139

'You'll like the South side Jo. It's different. Perhaps we'll move there one day.'

They got a bus from the place where a statue of Nelson had once stood. A landmark, there had been commotion when it had got blown up. Outrage and disclaim ensued, with letters to the press. Anglophiles mourned its loss, no Nelson looking down on them, a slight to Merrie England, the city wasn't the same. Dublin was proud of being peace-loving.

'I'm sick of snow', Hope said.

'It's pretty when we're indoors. Tell me about the statue getting blasted.'

John looked annoyed, disliking any reference to hooliganism. Thoughtless damaging was uncivilized. Sometimes he was at a loss to understand his countrymen, their politics affronted him. It was better to remain uninvolved, aloof. He believed in freedom to develop and express the spirit. The basic premise must be right.

'What started all the bother? Why is there hatred, fighting?'

John said that unrest and friction was often indigenous to Northern areas. The South were easy-going. The weather, industry, temperament contributed to situations. It was a matter of geographical location.

'But, John, isn't it all one god, a loving god. Why fight?'

'It's all exaggerated. The media are to blame. Don't talk about it. The trouble is only in the North, not here', said Hope.

'But John lived there, Hope.'

'We're Southerners. We love peace.' The word North discomforted him. He'd been thankful to be assimilated into Dublin, Dublin was famed for hospitality, had welcomed his wife and sister-in-law, adopting them. He loved to walk her streets, admire the Liffey. He'd quickly moderated his Derry accent, could hardly remember any other life, thanks to his cousins in Terenure. As a student he had lived with them. He looked forward to showing Jo another Catholic family where there was calm, where every child was loved. Hope doted on them. Though Mrs. Dunn was excellent, an ally under their roof, befriender, she lacked ideals, her outlook was limited due to peasant origin. His cousins, too, were simple, living to the faith. A child reared in the faith was safe from wrong. He liked the open manners of the English, deploring their lack of religion. England needed teaching.

140

The wind blew drifts of snow along the street. He was glad he'd bought a warmer coat for Hope, of camel hair. As the bus crossed the bridge he saw the water, leaden-quiet, not reflecting the gulls, the buildings or heads of pedestrians above the parapet, and felt pride akin to ownership. If he had sons they'd go to Trinity. The truth was what he aimed for, teaching appreciation of words written in truth. He admired the writers who wrote of Dublin with involvement. City for scholars. He sat behind the sisters, watching them. Their sensitive English faces lightened as they talked, they snuggled into their coats. He'd bought them knitted caps to pull down over their ears, though he never felt the cold, wore only a scarf over his heavy pullover. Shivering was for women. Their healthy skin and noses shone. He liked their long straight hair hanging from the woolly camel-coloured caps. Hope pointed at buildings. It was vital that Joanna noticed everything. Dublin was historic. Joanna harped too much on troubles and violent aspects of things.

Shops on the South side were expensive. No makeshift twirls of Christmas paper in their windows, Grafton Street was thinking of spring, and gold was the season's colour. Plaster models in Easter hats bent over toadstools or hatching eggs. Rabbits danced from threaded string, stretched invisibly. Seen through falling snow these wonders looked amazing. 'See Switzers Jo. Not cheap. One of our most exclusive shops. The fashion here isn't extreme.'

In Dublin girls wore bras, and mini skirts were few. There were displays of hand-loomed tweed, dresses of Irish lace, Celtic brooches and carved wooden objects for the home. In Grafton Street a dog or a child was displayed with pride. Leads had name-tags, reins had bells as dog or child was lifted from a car to be led into a teashop or a church. The Pro-Cathedral was near, and never empty, you stopped in for a prayer while shopping. Observance was in the blood in spite of fasting being relaxed. A waitress would still remind you if you ordered meat on Friday. A man counted fivers into the hand of a girl in a white mac. She held a winter plant, its red petals poking from the folds of florist's paper. A prostitute was something unknown here, no erotic literature was displayed in case of unchaste longings. Hope wanted Joanna to like everything, to approve. She longed for her first communion, prefaced by confession.

'How can you look forward to confession? What will you say?' Hope would have to kneel in a wooden box and whisper happenings into the ear of a stranger.

'I'll prepare for it. You make a list of sinning. The priest calls you daughter.'

'The worst sin is taking life in my view. Praying is all very well. Look at them in the North.'

'Steady now, Joanna.' John didn't want the conductor noticing them. Religion and politics were better discussed at home, behind your own front door. People would always watch and listen to the sisters. Joanna, less sure than Hope, was just as accustomed to being noticed. Politics were safe in large gatherings. By the gates of Stephens Green a placard said "Vote O'Regan. O'Regan will bring peace". A small crowd gathered, stamping the heaped snow round the railings to compressed chunks. A meeting in the open was a draw, as powerful as the attraction of racing or downing pints. A child on a tricycle stared at the placard before thudding his wheels back and forth against the railings. His mother beckoned to him to join her and the pram where a fat toddler sat encased in wool. It was rare to see a pram containing more than one child on the South side, or groceries piled round the babies' knees. Little children pushed dolls' prams or rode bikes, though now, because of the snow, there were few out on the streets. Inside the Green the trees were bare of leaves, birds sat quietly on the twigs. Traffic had been warned to use fog lights, because of the snow. "Vote O'Regan. O'Regan is your man" was shouted through a loudhailer. 'Poxy lot' the conductor muttered. O'Regan was for non-violence, for peace at any price. O'Regan blamed the soldiers, the blacks,foreign agents from over the water for any argument.

'Wait till you meet the cousins', Hope said. You only had to see how well the people lived. Red holy lights showed blessedly through parlour curtains. Houses were named "Stella Maris" or "St. Aloysius Rest" The priests and nuns were Ireland's royalty.

'I hope these cousins of yours won't bash out my brains with their rosaries. Religion here is overdone.'

John ignored this. The babbling of heathen was better disregarded. Hope said that the cousins went to convents, that Joanna should watch her talk. The family was strict.

'What have I said wrong?'

142

'Just watch it. You'd better say as little as possible. Above all do not swear.'

'I never swear. I never did. It's you. You swear. You don't want me to be a deaf mute by any chance?'

'I don't swear now. Watch your talk and keep your mouth shut.' Swearing was for the immature, blasphemy could count as sin.

The conductor was sorry when they left him at the request stop in Terenure, near which was Cousin Luke's house. Hope had persevered to be accepted by them, she didn't want Joanna ruining it. At first sight of Hope they'd felt uneasy. Cousin Luke had asked John privately if the girl was in the habit of taking a glass, if she was steady. He didn't trust them painted, the ones with know-all eyes. Hope looked a fast one, he'd heard tales of London. A man's life was his own, but carousing spelled ruin to a girl's soul. Not Catholic. But then, when Hope had looked at him and told him that she sang, loved Schubert, looked forward to her classes in religion, Cousin Luke had been quite affected. He'd blown his nose while she confided that she wanted to be a Catholic like all of his family, that she longed to make her first confession. Her soul would be remade, scraped clean, an old utensil renovated. He'd bought the inlaid pearl book, written "To our daughter Hope" and given it with the beads that he'd saved from a pilgrimage to Rome. They looked on John as a son, now he'd brought them another girl. He was confident she'd put away her paint and take to their ways. He congratulated John. A malleable girl he could hardly help from petting. He could understand John's rush, though marriage was a serious business. London's loss was Dublin's gain, a wife was asset to a teacher. He was proud of John's success. He felt curious to meet the younger sister.

The hall smelled of fried eggs and woollens hot from the ironing board. The mother left the kitchen to greet them with hands that felt waterlogged. The tips of her split-softened nails were frayed, the fingers slithered from their grip. Because of always being tired she was less friendly than Cousin Luke. Perpetual tiredness and fatigue was her main topic. She touched Joanna. 'Wash, wash, wash, that's my life. I make them turn their collars but it's nothing but shirts and wash, wash, wash.'

Her childrens' necks had raw marks from so much starch. They had mealy expressions. Their mother was a cowed woman. Cousin Luke

143

had the authority, he called the tune, wanting clean shirts, fried food and more children. Joanna watched Hope currying favour, offering to change the baby, put out cups, peel potatoes. Beneath her new freedom Hope still was childish, fond of approval, wanting to be loved, looked after. She couldn't stand alone. Since Miss Delicate had fallen, Joanna had become accustomed to being without an older person to lean on, or to think about. Since the night of Mallory's death she'd stopped imagining a close relationship with a man. Men terrified her. Not John, who treated her with brotherly affection. He teased her about her slow progress with the typing and liked to hear about the school in Putney. He liked hearing about Miss Delicate. Miss Delicate had determination. He was sorry that she'd never walk. He included Jo in everything where possible. At night when the bedroom doors were closed she sometimes heard Hope cry. Not a call of fear but ecstacy, half moaning as she called his name. She supposed this was a love call and that married people did it. Cousin Luke's head was bald and polished pink, like old ham. His ear lobes hung largely.

Upstairs, in the large bathroom, hands were washed before the meal. A pulley of underwear dripped over the tub, for though Cousin Luke had a good job, manager of a hardware store, the children kept the budget tight. No washing machine or luxury, though the house was large. Floor covering was sample squares of carpet stitched together. The only perks Luke got were bags of fertiliser and tulip bulbs. Another child arrived before they had time to buy extra comforts. The back windows were still curtainless after twelve years of marriage, you could see the rows of beans and cabbages that Luke grew. He was a steady husband, the mother never ceased to give thanks for it. She might be tired of washing and birth but a steady husband was a blessing. He handed her the wages on a Friday, tended his vegetables with fertiliser and attended to his married rights. The hand basin was big enough for several pairs of hands. Washing was ceremonious, the soaping, finger paddling, the patting on the roller-towel. Now Hope was a Dubliner she never forgot to wash her hands after the lavatory, rinsing self-righteously. In Cousin Luke's toilet was a notice "Now, please wash your hands" as well as "Your lies killed Christ". The mother spoke breathily, barely above a whisper. She told Hope not to bother helping with the clothes. She washed each morning plus usually a load at night. Hope was not to

144

think of it. She refilled the basin for another set of hands. She said to Joanna that likely she'd be delighted about it being twins.

'It will be a novelty I suppose. If Hope is pleased then I am.'

'Twins run in your family? You have a history of them?'

'Not to my knowledge.'

'Did you not ask your parents were there any twins?'

'I haven't set eyes on my father for donkey's years. They are divorced.'

The mother drew in her breath as the basin filled up. She swilled the flannel. She turned to arrange the rubber toys, the duck, the flat-bottomed boat and the fish whose colours were faded and had lost his squeak. A strand of thin hair fell across her neck. She was limp with the horror of it. She put the duck, the boat and fish in a line along the bath. Divorce was sin, an alien thing. Divorce was for Hollywood stars and those hell-bent. Divorce was not respectable at all. Such talk must be kept away from Luke who thought the sun shone from out of Hope. Hope was his shining light. No wonder she'd not been keen to mention her father. Divorce was mortifying, worse than alcoholism or mental deficiency in the family.

'So you see I can't ask him. I don't know where the man is. Somewhere in Florida when we last heard, wasn't it, Hope?'

Hope nodded. The mother scrubbed a pair of cheeks, running the cloth behind the child's ears, inspecting eyes and nostrils.

'Your Mammy is alone so?' she managed to ask.

'Yes. I told you. He went and left her.'

'He went his way. Your Dadda went his own way? Was that the way of it?' Put like that it wasn't quite so desperate. The sisters' father had gone his own way, being a man of strong temperament. Husbands did this thing, they left their families and behaved in ways often best not brought to light. For such a mother priests and parish workers had great sympathy. A wife had no redress, victim of heaven's decree. If her man went his own way only the holy saints and a bit from the poor box could help her. Poor poor English mother left on her own with two.

Cousin Luke intoned a grace over the scrubbed faces and hands of his family. He loved a full table, a visible sign of a happy marriage. There was no more pleasing sight for a man to see than those heads, first bent over in prayer, then bent over Mammy's frying. He loved to

145

see Hope with them, one of the saved. And now John had brought the sister too.

'And how is your own mother', he asked Joanna, 'from Putney, London, is it not?'

'As far as I know it's Putney. She's moving eventually. Away from Putney.' She didn't like mentioning Putney, not at table. Time didn't lessen some associations. Place-names haunted you.

'Lecturing? Is it a teacher she is? A teacher the likes of John?'

'No. Doctor, actually.'

'Doctor? You didn't tell us, Hope. You never said your mother was a doctor.'

'A specialist. Our mother is a Family Planning specialist.' Joanna wished Hope wouldn't leave all the talk to her. John was as bad. Once inside Cousin Luke's door both had become silent.

'Family what?' Cousin Luke's face and the top of his head turned puce. His breathing could be heard the other end of the long table. He pulled his upper lip over his long teeth.

'Another piece of black pudding Luke? I made extra, just for you.' The mother restrained herself from raising her hand in a blessing, stretching instead to the serving spoon and dish of eggs with pudding done up with mash. She'd read of it in magazines. Family Planning was not having babies when you were married. Family Planning was what the Protestants did. Family Planning was mortal sin. The doctor mother was a sinner of the most damnable die. Divorced as well. She was the worstest kind of sinner, she made money from her sinning, and went on doing it. Planning Families was planning sin.

The silence was broken by Luke's breathing and the sound of black pudding being munched. He swilled tea round his mouth. He looked at Hope, her hair all round her face, hunched over her plate. The unfortunate creature.

'They do things differently in England', he said at last, vowing that none of his should ever set a foot there. The devil raged in London. No one could say he was not a reasonable man, but that mother's work was worse than murder or walking the pavements for no good purpose. There were two sides to every question. John had gone over there and come back with Hope. Hope had been saved. Now, here was the younger one, come to stay, and possible future convert. That was the way to see it. Two sinners extricated.

146

'Joanna's never going back. She's staying here.' It was Hope's first remark.

'I'm learning typewriting. I'm nearly seventeen', Jo said. Seventeen, she hadn't learnt calm, hadn't learnt the art of relating. No boyfriend, no real friend at all.

'She likes it, don't you, Jo? She's getting on alright. Once she has the skill I have some contacts.' John felt a mixture of shame for his cousins' lack of sophistry and pride in their probity. Their Catholic fervour was phenomenal. This table had witnessed many thousand graces, born many thousand fries on its oak panels and still more thousand cups of tea. They'd thrown their doors open to him when he moved south. A smile, a prayer, a fry and tea were a certainty at Cousin Luke's. It was thanks to this household that Hope laid her table in the same way, pronounced the long A in Amen and Holy Mass, bowing her long thin neck. She didn't gobble any more and kept a clean sweet home like that of Cousin Luke. He'd be delighted if that lovely body of hers produced children as healthy as his little cousins. Of course, with him as head, his children would succeed academically. Cousin Luke, a simple soul, had never shone scholastically. There'd be no lack of brilliance in the Conquest family, he'd see to that.

'I'm fond of poetry', Joanna said. 'I wouldn't mind a job in publishing. In a small way of course.'

'A poem is an excellent thing.' Cousin Luke's colour slowly receded. He took another mouthful of pudding. He could see the snow still falling through a crack of the curtains. Snow was such pure stuff, he liked it, particularly when snug in the heart of his family. It was hard to know what made a poem excellent, except that some of them came in books. On the whole a poem was best kept for simple hymns or rhymes in greetings cards. It was to be hoped her poems weren't impure. That mother touring the streets and lecture halls of London with her hell-broth messages could have had no good influence on a poem. Better forget poetry. Typing classes, now, that was money well laid out.

After the tea was eaten the rosary was said, kneeling in a half circle round the fire facing the crucifix over it. The face looked like Mallory. Each child had a rosary. Beads were handed down the family like clothes, except for Cousin Luke's own, bought on the pilgrimage

147

to Rome. They had glass ones, pink, blue, orange, threaded on weak chains that broke, and medals that turned green with verdigris. The mother prised the broken links with scissors, mending them. A rosary was blessed, you mended it, it couldn't be thrown out. A blessed object when no longer useful must be burned by fire. The younger babies had a heap of beads to turn over on the floor. Joanna watched and listened to the clittering beads passing through large and small fingers, listened to the click of loose ones on the boards. Cousin Luke's beads fell with a heavier, more important sound. John called the decades. Saturday was the day for the glorious mysteries. The Resurrection, Ascension, the Descent of the Holy Ghost, the Assumption of the Blessed Virgin and her Coronation. The repeated Hail Marys were monotonous. It was a strange and holy jargon. She watched Hope ape the younger ones. Hope was a parrot at Cousin Luke's. She copied their praying, eating, washing habits, she smiled and abased herself. She wanted children like Cousin Luke's, all with saints' names. She wanted her home to smell of fried eggs, washed wool and have an open fire where religious objects could be suitably got rid of when worn out. Their visit had been spent in eating, praying and hand-washing.

The three thought with pleasure of the orange home waiting on the North side. The sisters pulled down their caps and stamped their boots, waiting at the bus stop. The streets were nearly empty. The placard for O'Regan was leaning against the wall of a pub, the people were gone home.

'Did you have to keep crossing yourself so much Hope?'

'It's an outward reminder. A reminder of Christ's death', Hope said righteously.

'I find it quite offensive. An unpleasant souvenir.' Crucifixes were everywhere, on buildings, round necks and swinging from the ends of beads. The religion of the Irish had started with violence.

'Not so much bloodshed as a consecration, Jo. A witness to faith. Faith is grace from God. You accept on trust.' John liked to see Jo questioning, the matter concerned her, she cared.

'It's just too much to swallow. Mysteries, virgins breeding, bodies rising. I can't accept it. I must be free, not bound by a code of another's making.'

'Faith holds a home together. I'd hate to think what I'd do without my religion. I'd be lost, especially when in any trouble, you turn to god.' John said.

'I'm happier than I ever was, knowing that I'll be a catholic soon.'

'I'm alright as I am.'

13

'Dear Mrs. Conquest and Miss Greenham. This is to inform you that
your mother, Dr. Margaret Greenham is in Ward C of the McIntosh
Block, having been admitted two weeks ago suffering from acute
asthma, necessitating the use of an oxygen tent. She did not want you
informed earlier. Now, she has requested me to write. She does not
want you to consider returning. I feel I should warn you that in her
weakened state her condition is still serious. Should you wish for
further details I will be happy to inform you.'

'Dear Ho and Jo. Guess its near your time so thought Id write these
few lines you done right to marry John how do you like being a mum
it is a giggle is it not. I read in the paper about the midgets they were
found dead in there basement they were quite bald there hair was
wigs they had on there tap shoes so suppose it was there hearts.
Where is the god of love in that? Surprise surprise I'm on for another
keep smiling love Lilian Pratt.

The sisters discussed the two letters in worried voices. Because of
their feelings of sadness and guilt the orange kitchen seemed less
cosy. The sweet gents had died a lonely death, they never would get a
letter from Marylebone, never would feel their warm affection. Their
waving hands, their smiles as they said goodbye before leaving the
Camp had been the last of them. Addresses, promises exchanged had
come to this. They'd stay for ever in the past, a memory of the strange
Camp world. The news about their mother was a bombshell.

'Was it shock at hearing about the twins do you think? Or rabbit
fur? Which was it Hope?'

'It may be both. It explains why she never wrote to me in answer.
John thinks she must be warped. A life of frustration has warped her
spirit.'

'Dreadful.'

'We knew about the rabbit affecting her. It was unkind. We should
have been more compassionate.'

'She always had asthma, Hope. Before the rabbit.'

'He made it worse. I used to hear her wheezing. I laughed. I was glad. I never thought she'd end in hospital under oxygen.'

'It doesn't say she'll die. She's strong. Should I go back to see her? I'd rather not.'

'John would say you should. He'd say fly back and find out how she is.' John, busy with teaching his English class, would be saddened when he heard about the gents. He'd pray for them. He'd be concerned about his mother-in-law who had neglected her daughters so badly. He believed that concern without action was wasted emotion. He'd say Joanna ought to go from duty.

'John isn't my conscience or mentor. I decide things myself.' John, when told, might even want her flown over to the orange flat to recuperate. He'd try to bend her will, he'd speak of hatred being like a cancer and love being a duty that healed everything. Hope needed her, especially that day for her Clinic visit. She said they shouldn't mention the two letters until they had absorbed the sorry news, and been to the Clinic.

Hope relied on her a lot. She needed helping off the bus. The stairs made her pant. She had black circles under eyes. Joanna held her clothes while Hope was being examined by the doctor, held her urine samples and collected the green iron pills and calcium for her. As well as this the other nervous patients got reassurance from her, she had the knack of soothing them. Newcomers were prone to agitation when confronted with internal examination or the mention of their monthly cycle. The taking-off of knickers for a stranger went against the grain. They clutched their medals to their fattening breasts and wailed, invoking the patron of mothers. Stories went round about babies born with hooves. The sighting of a mouse could mean a furred child. Things could go wrong, breast milk could sour. There was the humiliation of waiting in a line with only a hospital gown between you and the world. It was wanton. The doctor asked them mortifying questions. Only for the nurse being a nun you'd need to confess it. The hospital had a name for excellence in childbirth. It was a consolation that your body was needed for a student to practise on. For these timid ones Joanna had compassion. 'Don't worry, it is nature. You haven't a disease. My sister is getting twins and happy as a lark. It's her first time as well.' It was rewarding being useful. If she

151

got tired of waiting for Hope with the rest she read copies of *Homes and Gardens*. These were stacked on an oak table in the waiting room. There were articles on how to keep a man's love, and beautiful sitting rooms. It was difficult to stop thinking now about the gents, dead from dancing. She heard their voices in her mind, the tones high-pitched, the words clipped. It would have pleased them to know about Hope's twins. They had adapted to their stunted situation, set their own standards and shown love towards her and Hope. She asked her as they travelled homewards when the Clinic was over. 'What must it be like Hope, to really love someone?'

Hope said that it was putting someone first, being constantly in each other's thoughts, wanting their good. John loved her more than life, he told her every day. She worshipped him. He made her feel safe. There wasn't anything he wouldn't do for her except resign his faith. She spoke of the importance of duty to your soul, you had to guide it into heaven. John would die for her, but he wouldn't risk his chance of heaven. After death their souls would reunite.

Mrs. Dunn liked to hear about the Clinic visits. She was knitting things for Hope. Round shawls in pairs, not much larger than doilies, and boottees. Now that the walk to Moore Street tired Hope she had to take reports about her to the women who wanted news. The girls were missed. The women sent their prayers and, once, pigs' trotters as a remedy for Hope's ankles. Pigs' trotters were good for swellings. Hope couldn't wear her boots now and had to rest her feet on cushions in the night. Sitting listening to the clever well-bred girls talking about vitamins and doctors was better than a play for Mrs. Dunn. She knew it would be triplets, she'd engage on that. Don't mind the doctors talk. Triplets were a certainty. Mrs. Dunn had always had a devotion to the Trinity and good news came in threes. She'd had a bet down Moore Street. A friendly group of them ran a little sweep and waited for the event. Hope said that triplets weren't possible, where would they put three? The X-rays didn't lie. Mrs. Dunn said don't mind them, she'd put her money on three. When Hope laughed, her eyes became less puffy, the black circles less noticeable. She never forgot to put on perfume before John arrived and brush her hair. His step, his key in the lock, were passwords to their together world, their touching loving world of two. After he had kissed Hope he remembered to ask Joanna how the typing was

152

progressing. Mrs. Dunn liked watching her practice at the kitchen table. 'Now is the time for all good men to come to the aid of the party.' With Mrs. Dunn saying 'Good girl yourself'.

After Mrs. Dunn had gone and they had eaten, John read them a sombre essay by Graham Greene. Later she heard Hope and John praying from their orange bedroom. They kept their voices low out of consideration for her pagan state. The prayers were long, continuing after she fell asleep. She had another bad dream, again about the swimming pool. Lil Pratt and children, the little gents, splashed at the surface of the water. 'Don't go Hope. Don't go, I trust and love you. Don't, I love you', she yelled. She woke up with her knee hurting her, not knowing where she was. She was cold. It was dark, she wasn't in her bed, she wasn't alone.

'Great heavens what are you screaming for? What is it? Why are you out of bed?' John switched on his bedside light. His beads, looped over the shade, cast freckled shadows over the large bed.

'She's walking in her sleep again. She often used to', said Hope. She told Jo not to worry, she'd walked into their room. The mound made by her feet on cushions matched the mound of her stomach. She looked comfortable, blinking in the freckled light.

'I . . . I didn't mean . . . ' Joanna's mouth felt dirty. She'd woken them, was standing now on John's side.

'Alright alright. You only sleep-walked, Jo. You had a dream and got out of bed. I knew you used to do it, Hope told me. We'll have to cure you. Don't worry.'

Her knee had banged into their door. Bad dreams and sleep-walking were a hangover from childhood. John said that the typing was too much for her, she should relax. Hope needed her sleep, they didn't want Hope upset or tired just now, did they? And he guided her back to where she belonged in the twins' room. He pulled her blankets up gently and said again that they must only think of Hope.

She tried to hear if they were laughing. Being laughed at was worse than being prayed about. Each time she shut her eyes disaster flicked into her mind. Miss Delicate lying on the concrete in the letter O with blood on her forehead. Fur of a rabbit being breathed. A toilet bolted to conceal a sad-eyed, hanging man. Muck-strewn bed-clothes out of sight. Then she heard Hope crying from the door across the passage.

John left the room. 'Keep still, Hope. Keep very still. I'll be but a minute.'

He told Joanna he was going to telephone, that Hope was in pain. That she should go to her and comfort her.

He took his scarf, unlocking the door. He had the hands of a priest. Kindness showed in people's hands. He was the only man she felt no fear of . . . He said don't let Hope see she was worried.

'Where does it hurt you, Hope?'

'My Back. There's been some blood. I don't want them now. I can't leave John.'

'But I'll look after him. Don't be silly, Hope, you won't be long away.'

When he came back he said the ambulance was coming.

'I'll walk, I'll walk down', she said to them. The men had navy caps and chit-chatted. Reassurance was their stock-in-trade. They made a chair for her with their crossed hands, told her she was gorgeous, that she wouldn't find the time till she was a mother. With twins she'd soon know what marriage was all about. Twins weren't so plentiful this weather. So gorgeous was she that only for the fact she was a married woman they'd run off with her. She was an angel from heaven's gates, so stop creating do. The stairs were difficult. Used to contriving, they had padded their wrists to ensure that they didn't become bloodied.

'Alright Ma, not your turn this time. Wait till you get your twins.'

' 'Tis triplets. Triplets. Lay you three to one', cried Mrs. Dunn and threw another holy card onto Hope's knees.

The east wind blew scraps of snow-rimed paper against the ambulance doors. The men said they couldn't take Joanna. Strictly speaking, they shouldn't take the husband. They told her to go back to bed. It would be the afternoon, at least, before there was any news. The wind blew a corner of scarlet blanket off Hope's hands. She tried to stretch to her, she must have her sister, didn't they understand?

Mrs. Dunn and Joanna were left in the hallway. Mrs. Dunn jabbered about St. Jude. The saints cared, would see Hope through the triplets. Her Moore Street friends had started a novena.

Joanna didn't listen. Her mother in Putney might be dying, the gents were in the ground, Miss Delicate was crippled, Mallory, cause of the situation, was a suicide unmourned. 'I'm going to the hospital. I'll walk.'

154

14

From the passage outside the ward she heard Hope shouting.

'It can't be time for the birth. I don't feel ready. Where's Jo?'

'The baby decides, not you, Mrs. Conquest. A baby makes its own mind when to appear. You're making a commotion.'

'It's twins you realise? It's not a baby. Twins. Where's Jo?'

'Now, Mrs. Conquest, please, don't make such a commotion. A baby is a drink of water compared to some complaints. Have patience.'

'Hope darling, the Sister knows your case. They know it's twins. Why won't you settle down?'

'John please . . . get Jo.'

'You have a nice corner bed, Mrs. Conquest. Why don't you settle down in it?'

'Because I've got to have my sister.'

'I'm here, Hope. Here I am.'

'Where've you been? Jo, you've got to stay with me.'

'Mrs. Conquest, please, this is a ward in a hospital. You cannot take your sister into bed with you, whatever next? Let go, let go of her, Mrs. Conquest please.'

'Hope darling, that's enough now. Come, where's your courage?'

'Here comes the Doctor. Outside, everybody, please. No visitors around the bed. This way Mr. Conquest, and er . . . Miss Conquest, here comes Doctor.' The Doctor would settle the new patient's tricks. Everybody had respect for the Doctor.

Voices muttered from other beds. The new one was over-doing it. Whisht. 'Lie down there, Missis, before you have the child in your knickers.'

Joanna followed John, leaving the white-gowned staff round Hope. She'd never seen John looking white. The whiteness of his face made his hair and eyes look blacker. It wasn't what he'd expected. The ward shocked him. There was little dignity about these women wearing

155

hospital nightwear, their eyes weary with pain. They were used to having their ante-natal rest disturbed. The place was full of pain. Pain present and pain to come. The plaster statues placed at either end, the Virgin and the Infant Child of Prague were there to give encouragement, their painted eyes and lips enjoining stoicism. The old timers put a brave face on things. They asked the nurses to get them weak tea, cracking bawdy exchanges. 'May your troubles be little ones.' 'My man's too often hard up.' They told John not to worry, that his missus would get gas and air from the contraption, that is, when she'd suffered good and well.

The two waited at the oaken table with the copies of *Homes and Gardens.* Nuns with beads swinging under their aprons rushed about, their eyes blankly calm as the statues. John and Joanna were offered thin biscuits on a tray, with coffee. Relatives of twins were special. Soon the day staff would come on.

'I scared her, John. Is it my fault that she's here?'

He said it wasn't so. The twins were due. Hope was in good hands, God would care for her. He clasped his hands between his knees, bending over as he sat, having put down his coffee cup. She couldn't remember any kind of prayer. 'Wunwun won a space race, Tutu won one two.' 'Now is the time for all good men to come to the aid of the party.' He said she ought to walk about, it would stop her worrying so. He'd stay at the table, in case of being wanted.

In the passages, wearing dressing-gowns, were patients who had been ordered to move about. Moving was assistance in the early stages, moving kept the mind occupied, reduced the tension. A nun called to them. 'Keep moving. Walk about.' Underneath the dressing gowns they had on shifts with broken tapes. They prayed, ticking off the Aves on their beads. Those without beads used their fingers. They looked suspiciously at Joanna. The nun asked which ward she was looking for, smiling coldly. Joanna hated Dublin, hated these people. She'd never have a child.

When she got back to the oak table a man in a mask was talking to John. The tightness of the mask pushed against his eye sockets, making him menacing. He spoke of their reluctance to speed nature's process, to interfere. Sometimes it was necessary. Doctors had to decide. The patient was excitable. In such cases surgical manipulation was warranted. She was narrow.

'Sanctus, Sanctus, Sanctus', sang the nuns from the chapel. Devotions continued throughout birth, beyond death. Up one passage, down another, the dressing-gowned figures tramped, intent on their own pain. More coffee, more thin biscuits. She hated Dublin, she'd never have one. 'Sanctus, Sanctus, Sanctus.' 'Keep moving, move about.'

'I seen you at the Clinics. Your sister is the one with twins. Is it her time now? You told me not to worry, that it's natural, you comforted me, you're here again.' The new mother who had gone green at the prospect of examination said it was a sign from heaven that Joanna was there, to walk the passage with her. She said her name was Carmel, that she'd never forget Joanna.

'It's girls. Two little girls', John cried, rushing towards her. Twin girls. It was all over. Hope was over it.

She asked to see her but the sister said only the husband, she must stay outside. She took them to another ward, post-natal, place of calm after exhaustion, relief after pain, place of thanksgiving after safe delivery. The air had a milky smell, the face on every pillow wore an air of achievement as they looked at the bundles lying in the baskets by them, bundles to kiss and coo over. This was the best part, the part you enjoyed, savoured, you'd completed the course, you rested. It was a moment of worship before the world of hospital routine, of husbands, families, bills pushed in again. Curtains were still drawn round Hope, who'd been sedated.

'Are you the twinnies' Auntie? Come, take a peek. They can't be with the Mammy yet. Too small. They're in the Special Care. Look through the window. See?'

They lay with shut eyes. Their cheeks were plum-blue. Their noses slanted sideways like Mallory's. Their heads were bulgy-skulled, a little like the gents'. They looked frail, sleeping soundly, isolated for being surgically induced and small, oblivious of drama. Because of these she'd followed Hope to a country of dreamers and violence in the North.

'They have the Dadda's nose. A great look of their Da.'

John saw them later, looking through the glass with luminated eyes, examining each detail visible outside the blanket. He couldn't wait to start showing them the way to live. His children, his potential for a new world, world of the future. One had a redder face, accentuated bloom of hair. They bunched their fingers underneath their chins. A crusader, his twins were his reason for living, a second chance, they represented the casualties of warfare.

'Excuse me. I'd like to see my sister now. You see, she's used to me, she'll need me.'

'Now Auntie, no. The Mammy must have quiet. Only the Daddy can see her yet. Only fathers.'

Joanna asked if she could come that night. The Sister said that evening visiting was for fathers. They didn't have much time alone. Parents needed peace, this was their only chance. An Aunt must take her turn in the afternoon, a time for general visiting. She could come on Wednesday. An Auntie was a useful thing when mothers left a lot of mouths to feed at home, a lot that needed minding. This Aunt had no special purpose, so she must fit her visit in when suitable. She had little time for visitors in general, they took up space, left litter, brought snow in on their shoes. Flowers and fruit made extra work for the nurses, not to mention the ash-trays. A birth should be an organised affair and not a circus. This Auntie made the patient hysterical. That disturbance when she first arrived had been disgraceful.

John's mind was on a different plane as they travelled home. He planned his daughters' futures far ahead. He saw them opening their youthful mouths to receive the sacred wafer, he heard them sing cantatas. They would learn badminton and fill notebooks with neatly written sums that he would mark. They'd lead the rosaries, earn millions of indulgencies. His dynasty was headed by twin girls.

They heard Mrs. Dunn singing. 'Streets full of people, all alone. Roads full of houses, never home. Church full of singing, out of tune. Everyone's gone to the moon.' Her voice was ugly. John said she looked exhausted, made her sit with a cushion at her back. He boiled eggs for her, removing the tops neatly, sprinkling the revealed yolks with pepper, ready for her spoon. He said that a knob of butter made them delicious, touching her absently, stroking her hair and thinking about the Father's hour when he'd see his darling Hope and daughters again.

When he left Mrs. Dunn came. She'd heard the news, she'd lost her bet, no triplets after all. She wanted to hear if Hope's time had been a shocking one so that she could tell the women down Moore Street.

She wasn't interested in the twins, only in the manner of their coming.

'Induction? Holy God, that's bad. Induction does be a terrible misfortune.'

'Now that they're born I feel it's all an anti-climax. I feel worn out, Mrs. Dunn. I'm needed here I know. But . . . our mother isn't well in London. I'm so tired.'

Mrs. Dunn said that a mother's life was not one of roses. She'd seen many a mother jaded-looking. There were times when she was glad that Mr. Dunn was out of it and she alone in peace. Did Joanna have one of those icing cakes? A cake went down well with tea. She said Mr. Conquest was the lucky man to have a sister-in-law to fall back on, to iron, to cook and tidy. And when Hope was back home from the hospital Joanna could go back to London, England to care for her sick mother. It was great to be needed.

But when he came in again he said that Hope's temperature was up. That she was feverish, they'd put her in a single ward. His face looked wretched, he didn't eat the food she prepared. He said he had to get up early and call there before school. Joanna said that it was due to tiredness, that Hope always over-reacted. She poured his drink, sugaring it as Hope did, but he didn't drink. He went to bed without looking at the item in the English paper she had marked, about a derelict school in Putney waiting to be bought.

In the early hours they heard Mrs. Dunn calling up the stairs. The hospital had sent a note, to hurry Mister, it was urgent, the hospital the hospital.

'It's serious', he said. Though she knew.

Mrs. Dunn wailed after them that prayer worked miracles, prayer had prayed Hope to the door of the church. She'd never trusted twins. Twins had done a mischief to her English friend, worse, they'd lost her good money down Moore Street. She told Joanna to pray to any god she knew.

'If anything happens to my Hope I'll die. I shall not want to live. I'll die.'

'She's my life too, Joanna. D'you not think I don't feel the same way?'

'You don't understand. You're only a husband. We've always been together. She's my sister. If she goes I shan't want to live. I should have seen her. Then this wouldn't have happened. I know Hope. I know what she needs.'

He said she wouldn't die, this bad time would pass. The hospital people were clever, he had every confidence in the doctors. He put his arm round her in the taxi, considerate to her in his own extremis. The taxi took them down side-streets, throwing their knees together as they turned corners. Street-lighting was weak in the dawn-lighted sky and the driver cursed the snow. Snow caused ill-health, snow reduced the speed of travel, made journeying hazardous. Snow kept people home-bound. The weather lost him his livelihood. His St. Christopher medal kept tapping against his dashboard.

The Sister in the Isolation Block wore navy because she wasn't a nun. Her cap was tall, like the Ku Klux Klan, it quivered as she demanded to know the reason for information being withheld. Why hadn't she been informed of Mrs. Conquest's allergy to antibiotics? Time had been lost unnecessarily. An allergy should be reported, noted in the file. The case was unprecedented. Carelessness was something they could not afford; someone had been careless, failed to check the details. Time had been wasted.

'Please, what do you mean? My sister Hope is never ill. What allergy?'

'We haven't had a case of septicaemia in years. Infection had time to get established while we tried different drugs. We should have been alerted.'

'Hope is never ill. What is septicaemia?'

'She has a fever. A streptococcal infection.' The Doctor had been quite sharp about it, rightly so. Each minute counted with post-natal infection, when resistance was debilitated. The omission was reflection on her own administration. A patient's idiosyncrasies should be noted in the comments section of her file. Now the patient was unconscious.

John came out of the room. He said he couldn't make Hope hear him. He told Jo to go in.

'Hope. Hope, listen to me. It's me, Jo. Hope, stop that heavy breathing. Listen Hope, your eye is twitching. It's twitching. Stop. You know it's hideous, stop it. There's nothing wrong with you. It's just a thing called a strep. Hope, stop that eye and listen. It's strep, that's all. Hope, if you die I'll have to have those twins. You can't. I

160

can't bear my life without you. That Catholic stuff and all those cousins. The funeral, I can't. Hope stop that breathing. Be alright. Be alright Hope.'

'Auntie dear, you are not doing any good. Come now, please, Auntie, that's enough, this way, don't bump the bed.' She had no liking for the Auntie in the camel coat, now verging on dementia. But she was fond of the patient, that much was plain. A nurse should never be a judge, a nurse should heal. A nurse should be alerted about allergies. She told them that the crisis might take time. They were to wait downstairs. They would send for them as soon as there was any change. Death on the premises was so untidy, it made her feel quite vexed. So unnecessary. Death was an emotional and financial drain, particularly in a building designed for the dawn of life.

The two sat down again by the oaken table with the *Homes and Gardens*.

15

She felt like shouting. Hope liked things bright and warm and spacious. Hope never could stand boxing in. They'd put her in an oaken box, in darkness. She had no light, no warmth, no space. They'd covered her with flowers. Hope loathed roses, now she was covered in them. They wrapped her in a sheet, they closed her twitching eyes and covered her in roses. Her fishboned hands were folded, she couldn't move. John asked her if she wanted her name put by his on the wreath of small white flowers. Wedding flowers. She wouldn't. Hope loved meadow flowers, cow parsley, weeds that grew rank in meadows. A meadow flower had no place on a coffin in a chapel. Mrs. Dunn had sent the largest wreath.

John had made her swallow a tranquillising pill, to stop her crying louder than the cousins who filled the place. Like priests and nuns of varying heights they sobbed on their black raincoat-covered wrists. Mrs. Dunn was the noisiest. Her sobs represented the whole of Moore Street to whom she still owed money. Cousin Luke supervised the undertakers, his cheeks and bald crown bright with the effort of containing himself. The service must be conducted properly.

Weak sunlight shone on the party, lighting the dark clothes as they left the chapel. John walked by her, holding her. The priest shivered as he spoke of pain and sorrow bravely borne, of Hope in the flower of her youth and *requiem in pace*, the holy angels leading into paradise.

She felt like shouting. Hope wouldn't like the rattle of earth and stones, she hated being hindered. She felt John's hand. Hope wasn't there to be frightened, wasn't there to be followed, protected, copied. Hope had gone, she couldn't follow, couldn't stay within her shadow.

a Ross

String Horses